GIVEN TO THE BERSERKERS

THE BERSERKER SAGA
BOOK 4

LEE SAVINO

SILVERWOOD PRESS, LLC

FREE BOOK

GIVEN TO THE BERSERKERS

Captured to be a prize in the brutal Berserker Games...

My life changed forever when the Berserkers took me. These fearsome warriors must find women to keep their lethal rage at bay...and I am an ideal mate.

The Alphas decree that all warriors must compete in a series of Highland Games for my hand. Of all the giant warriors, two have caught my eye, but I have no choice. When the final match is over, I will belong to the ruthless victors. They will possess me fully. I can only hope they will be the two I could come to love...

Note: *Given to the Berserkers* is a standalone, full-length MFM ménage romance starring two huge, dominant warriors who make it all about the woman. Read the whole best-selling Berserker saga to see what readers are raving about...

PROLOGUE

"Muriel," someone was calling my name and tugging on my arm. I opened my eyes, squinting against my throbbing headache. "Wake up," my sister said in a trembling whisper.

"What is it, Fleur?" I groaned. "Did the fire go out? Where's Sabine?"

"She disappeared, remember? We have not seen her for a day and a night." Fleur was speaking, but I barely heard her as I sat up and stared through the bars of a cage. Where I expected the walls of our home and the stone hearth, there was only forest.

"What is this?" I whispered. We sat in the center of a wooden cage made of branches as tall as a man and twice as long, lined with fur pelts. Beyond the bars, figures moved around a bonfire. A few men accompanied by giant dogs.

Fleur huddled closer to me. "They came in the night," she whispered. "Do you remember? They burst into the hut and grabbed us."

"I remember." My head ached but I recalled the dark shapes looming over us. I'd leapt to my feet, wielding a small knife my older sister Sabine made me carry. One of the warriors had caught the blade in his hand.

"Careful," he had laughed, wrenching the weapon from me even as blood dripped from his palm, "this one is a fighter. She has a little tooth."

"Get away from me," I'd shrieked. My defiance lasted as long as it took for one of the huge warriors to catch and force me down. I struggled on the floor, craning my neck to look back at Fleur. My twin sister was often sick, and weaker than I was. She'd shrunk back on the bed when three warriors converged on her. "Leave us alone!"

"Be quiet, and we won't hurt you." The warrior binding my wrists had covered my head with a sack and hefted me up. We were moving, moving, out of the hut and into the night. I'd screamed and struggled with all my might. The warrior carrying me slung me down, and—

Blackness. I remembered nothing more.

"What happened?" I asked my sister without taking my eyes off the men in the clearing. The huge warriors were cutting down more trees and adding logs to the fire.

"I don't remember much after they came in and took us. I must have hit my head."

"The man struck you so you slept," Fleur said. "But I stayed awake the whole time. They carried us here, faster than any man can run. I know you won't believe me..."

Fleur often had visions and dreams during the day, fantastical things she shared only with me. Often she saw things that weren't real, and asked me about them. With my help, she didn't speak of things that no one else saw. Otherwise, the villagers might call her fey, and kill her for it.

"I believe you," I said, holding her tighter. "This is real. This is happening." The men at the bonfire were more frightening when they stepped into the light than when they stood in shadow. Massive and muscular, they wore the garb of warriors and carried great weapons, from axes and bows, to daggers and swords. Though larger than any man I'd ever seen, they moved like predators, with smooth, quick grace. One of our captors walked out of the woods wearing only a loincloth, and carrying a giant log over his shoulder as if it weighed no more than a stick. He shrugged it off onto a growing pile, and joined a group that stood studying us in the cage. Amid the men roamed a few giant beasts that I thought were dogs, but for their size and the intelligence in their bright gold eyes.

Fleur and I huddled together amid this nightmare.

"Who are they?" I asked in despair. My teeth chattered, more with fear than cold.

"Wolves." Fleur pointed out two of the warriors standing guard. Not more than a minute passed without them glancing back at us. I noticed they seemed particularly interested in Fleur, and I squeezed her tighter. "See those two? They took turns carrying me. They told me a witch cursed them with great strength and speed, but with the curse came the rage of a ravening beast. I didn't understand until I saw one of them, that third one, there, turn from man into a wolf." The beast she pointed out was massive, bigger than any dog or wolf I'd ever seen. With its midnight fur and eyes shining in the firelight, it seemed a demon creature.

It hadn't stopped staring at Fleur.

"What do they want with us?"

"The warriors told me they have no women. They took us because they need mates."

I forced my disbelieving gaze from the giant beasts and warriors, to stare into Fleur's pale eyes. My normally pale sister looked even more wan and tired, with great circles under her eyes. But I knew she was telling the truth.

"How is this possible?"

"A prophecy foretold of a race of women they could mate with. Muriel... they have Sabine."

"She's here? Alive?" Our older sister had disappeared a few nights before. I sagged back onto the pelts, overcome with the first good news I'd had all night.

Fleur nodded and lay down with me. "They took her first. She's to mate with the two Alphas."

My forehead wrinkled. "Two of them?"

"They sometimes mate with women in pairs."

I closed my eyes. My head hurt again, and not because of the tender bump on my skull.

"Do you think she's all right?" I'd often been at odds with my older sister, but she'd always looked after us since our mother died. We had another sister, Brenna, older than all of us, but she, too, had disappeared.

"I think Sabine is fighting them. But they laughed about it and said that one way or another, the Alphas will tame her. And then..." Fleur's voice died away, but she didn't have to finish the sentence.

After Sabine was mated, it would be our turn.

Dawn came, and despite fear churning in my stomach and a raw feeling in my gullet, I dozed.

When I woke, the crowd of warriors had thinned. There were only three warriors left—the men who had carried Fleur, and their companion in wolf form.

Someone had left a skin of water just outside the bars. I waited as long as I could, but finally threaded my arm through the bars and took it. I sniffed it carefully but smelled no taint or poison. If these warriors had any reason to kill us, they could simply snap our necks. With that bleak reasoning, I didn't hesitate to drink from the skin.

The wind shifted and the smoke blew into our cage.

Fleur started coughing in her sleep. I moved to block the foul breeze, but she kept coughing. Her lungs had never been very strong.

Would that Sabine were here. She was smart and brave, and had a little magic. She would demand our captor bring her what she needed to make Fleur medicine, and would not stop standing up to them until we were all free.

I'd wrapped my arms around my legs and pressed my head to my knees., when a voice hissed close to my ear.

I raised my head and looked straight into golden eyes. A reddish wolf, so red I would've thought it was a fox if it hadn't been so large, sat panting not five handspans from where I sat within the cage.

I watched in wonder as a ripple of magic split the air. The beast's form shimmered, and then in place of the wolf crouched a man, naked but for a loincloth.

If Fleur had not explained the night before, I would've thought I was crazed or still dreaming, but the man looked real enough. He was young and sturdy, with a pale muscled chest and legs. The only resemblance to the wolf was his tousled red hair.

He grinned at me, and placed a finger to his lips, gesturing for me to stay silent. I glanced back at the warriors guarding us, and they all were focused on the fire. The smoke still blew in our direction. Turning my back on them, I nodded to the red-haired warrior. For some reason he didn't want to be seen, and his secret was safe with me.

His grin widened, displaying sharp incisors. He beckoned me closer.

For some reason, I obeyed, sliding on the pelts to tuck myself against the side of the wooden prison.

"Muriel?" His low voice was rough, but I recognized my name when he repeated, "Are ye Muriel?"

Gaping at him, I nodded.

"Are ye sure, lass?" he asked. "I have a message for Muriel, and I dinnae want to tell it wrong."

Licking my lips, I found my voice. "I am Muriel. Who are you? What's going on?"

"You've been taken by Berserkers, warriors cursed to live as beasts. Ye were stolen by the Lowland Pack. I am Fergus of the Highland Pack. My pack and this pack dinnae get along."

That explained his secrecy.

"You have a message for me?"

"Aye. My Alphas promise ye that ye will not be harmed. Soon ye will be free." He crept closer, crouching next to the bars. If I put my hand out, I could touch him.

"'Tis not wise for me to come out of hiding, but ye looked so sad. I wanted to reassure ye." He had a splash of light freckles across his nose.

"Thank you. That's very kind."

"I cannae stay long. I'm only here because the wind shifted. They willnae scent me as long as I'm downwind."

"Please, will you let us out?"

"I cannot. Not until I know ye are safe. Do ye know why you're in a cage?"

I glanced back at the fire, but our guards were still distracted. "To keep us from getting out?"

"No, to keep the monsters from getting in."

I wanted to close my eyes, lie down and go to sleep, and forget all this as a dream. Instead I studied Fergus. With his freckles and teasing manner, he could be a youth from my village, except for his rugged, handsome looks, and the magic that made him a wolf.

"Why did they take us? Why are we here?"

"They need brides."

Fleur had relayed the truth. I gripped the bars harder, and clenched my jaw to fight the tears.

Fergus looked stricken. "Now, lass, don't cry," the warrior crooned. ""Twill be all right."

"I don't know how...I don't know what to do."

"Help is on the way. I swear on my life, I will get ye out. Dinnae worry your wee head."

After a shuddering breath, I nodded.

"The wind is shifting. If they scent me, I'll be caught."

"Don't go," I begged.

He tilted his head. His shoulders were also dusted with freckles. "Ye aren't afraid of me, wee one?"

I didn't know what to say to that. "Please."

"I won't stray far. I'll make sure ye dinnae come to harm. This pack is dangerous, but the more unstable wolves have orders to stay away from ye."

He changed before my eyes, the masculine features distorting into the maw of a reddish wolf. I jerked back, but he was already gone, only the tremor of a leaf on a low-hanging branch evidence of where he had been.

I clutched at Fleur, but she was asleep, her cheeks wan and pale, her body shaking with coughs. Tears streamed out of my eyes--from the smoky air, I told myself. Not because I was afraid.

A warrior walked into the clearing. Pale and blond, he stood a head taller than the others, and towered over them when they bowed their heads.

"Arne, Erik," he greeted the men, and then the wolf. "Gunnr." He had a strange accent but spoke in a level, cultured voice. I'd almost think him a lord from some far off court, but he tilted his head and sniffed the wind, and I saw the predator in him.

"Alpha," the warriors greeted him, and his head jerked towards our cage.

"What is this?" the blond Alpha asked his men. "I smell a wolf. And not one of our pack."

"I smell it too." The warrior named Arne growled.

Fear flashed through me. They would track Fergus, and all would be lost.

I moved to the far side of the cage, opposite where I had sat with Fergus.

"Hey," I cried out. "You there." Gripping the branch bars, I tried to shake them. Fleur coughed again in her sleep, the perfect distraction.

The warriors' attention swung to me. My body was numb with fear, with cold, and now with anger.

"My sister is sick. She may be dying, if I cannot get her the herbs she needs."

The tall blond approached. Crouching he ducked his head to meet my gaze. His eyes were bright gold.

I waited for him to speak but he only cocked his head to the side.

"Did you hear me?" Fury supplied my words. "You captured both of us—and soon one will die. If she goes...I will make you pay." I did not know how. My cheeks were frozen from my old tears, or were they new?

"Threats for your captors?" the Alpha murmured. "I wonder what makes you so bold?"

"It's the enemy, Ragnvald," answered one of the guards —Erik. The second and third, in wolf form, stood at the forest edge, whining and pawing the earth where Fergus had been.

They paced along one side of the cage, and shivers worked up my spine.

"He was here. One of the Highland Pack. If we go now, we can track him."

I stared up into the leader's face, silently pleading.

"No," he said finally. "Let him go. If plans hold, the Highland Pack will not be our enemies for much longer."

I held the leader's gaze for a moment longer, then a sharp pain flashed in my head and I dropped my eyes. Power rolled through the clearing, beyond my mortal understanding, and the hair on my arms stood on end.

Fleur coughed again, breaking the spell.

"Please, my lord," I said. "My sister truly is ill."

"Do you know what will save her?" Erik asked in a harsh, almost guttural voice. He stalked towards the cage, eyes on Fleur's limp body. I shrank back, but the warrior stopped when his leader lifted a hand. Every muscle in Erik's body was taut, ready, as if at a word he would jump forward and rip apart the wooden structure.

"Yes," I gulped. "I can find the herbs to make medicine, if you let me out."

Fleur coughed and one of the wolves whined again.

"Alpha, please," Erik asked in a quiet voice. Sweat beaded on his forehead as he waited for his leader to give the order.

"Very well."

Erik reached out and sliced the bindings on one branch, so the side of the cage swung open.

"Take Gunnr and track our red intruder," Ragnvald continued. "When you catch him, do him no harm. Tell him I wish to meet under a branch of truce, to negotiate peace with his pack."

I did not breathe until the tense warrior was gone.

"Be at peace, Muriel," the Alpha said. "Your sister has

told me of you and your bravery. It seems even Fleur has charmed my men in less than half a day."

The bare blue sky called to me from beyond the wooden frame, yet still I hesitated. The Alpha beckoned. "Come forth, little sister. I am Ragnvald, Alpha of the Lowland Pack. I swear I will not hurt you."

"I am not your sister," I said.

"No," Ragnvald said, amused. "But when Sabine accepts her place at my side, you will be."

Heart beating fast, I ducked through the opening. The Alpha of the Lowland Pack swept out his hand, ushering me into my new life.

1

Nine moons later

I saw the wolf through the branches of the berry bush. Large and reddish with a white splash on his tail, he sat with his tongue lolling out, watching me.

With a smile, I turned back to the waiting branch and picked another handful of berries for my lunch.

A subtle wind lifted my skirts and brought a fresh, open scent--like the earth after spring rain. Leaves crunched under someone's foot--the sound too slight to notice unless I was waiting to hear it.

A pair of large, rough hands covered my eyes.

"Guess who," the Scottish brogue tickled my ear.

"Fergus," I whirled with a grin, and took in the young warrior, his handsome face and broad, muscled shoulders making my mouth water.

He stood bare-chested and unashamed, wearing nothing but a loincloth around his nethers. The pink in his cheeks was the only sign that he was affected by the slight chill.

I cleared my throat, ducking my head to hide my blush. "You should not be here...and I cannot see you like this."

"I cannae carry clothes wherever I go. My wolf likes to run unencumbered." His voice dropped to a seductive rumble, "Look at me, Muriel."

I did as he bid, raising my gaze to meet his clear blue ones. I watched in fascination as the magic within him took hold and turned his eye color to bright gold.

"I've missed ye, lass."

"And I've missed you," I whispered. Much had changed since we'd first met, exchanging names through the bars of the cage. My sisters and I lived with the Berserkers, less as captives and more as prized guests. Tensions between the packs had died down, but there were still treaties and negotiations. Fergus acted often as a go-between, and so even though I was with the Lowland Pack, I saw him often—but always in the presence of the Alphas or a few guards. Never alone, in a secret meeting, like this.

"Ye look well."

My skin tingled as his gaze swept up and down my form, hungry.

Clearing my throat, I sought for a change in subject. We had little chance to converse beyond a look, a small touch, a carefully worded greeting. The entire pack watched over my sister and me, for we were their hope for the future. But of all the giant, forbidding warriors, only Fergus could make me laugh with his antics, and the sly, silly comments that were innocent enough, but I knew were meant for me.

"I hoped you would find me today."

"Yes?" He took a step forward, eyes lit.

"Yes," I backed away, blushing. "I know I am not to speak to any of the warriors because I am unmated, but I wanted to speak to you."

"Well, then, lass." He kept moving forward, and I kept backing away. "What did ye want to say?"

No matter how much distance I put between us, he stalked me slowly. At last he cornered me against the berry bush. My heart beat faster, fluttering like a bird taking flight.

He raised his hand and offered me a white flower.

Warmth rushed through me. Smiling, I took hold of it by the stem. "I knew it was you." Lately, I'd found the little white flowers everywhere. A small token that could've been carried by a bird, or fallen from a tree, but when I found it on a stump in the clearing near our new home, or a rock in the stream where Sabine and I washed our clothes, I'd guessed it was a gift from the red wolf. "Thank you. It's beautiful. But I need to tell you...I wanted to warn you. You should not come so close to me. It's not safe."

He tilted his head, as if touched at my worry. "I dinnae care about my safety."

"I do. Please, Fergus. I don't want the others to find you here."

"They willnae catch me. I am small, yes, but I am fast when I'm the wolf."

I started to protest and he held a finger up, almost brushing my lips. "Do ye want to spend our time arguing?"

"No."

"Then let us speak of other things."

There was so much I wanted to ask him, so much I wanted to know. I often imagined him while I lay awake at night on my pallet, pressing the white flowers he left for me to my lips.

"Does it hurt to Change?"

"Not into the wolf. The beast, our Berserker form, is brought on by extreme emotion. That can be painful, if only because of the desire to fight and rip apart the very earth. But

we shall speak no more of becoming monsters." His voice
was light, but I knew he worried about the beast taking over
his mind. All Berserkers were once men who were cursed
with the magic of the Change. They could control the shift
from man to wolf, but after decades of fighting, they eventually lost control of their monstrous third form: the beast.

To me, though, Fergus was no monster. The red-headed
warrior could've been a boy from my village, grown up into
a man I could love. I'd always imagined such a suitor
courting me. We'd have a country wedding, and a sweet,
simple life with each other and our children.

My life had changed but I held onto my small, sunny
dream. Whenever I was with Fergus, I felt it could still come
true.

I swung off my cloak and wrapped him in it.

"Walk with me?" I invited. We weren't supposed to be
near each other. War could break out if we were found
together, but the pull between us couldn't be denied.

As we ambled along the woodland path in silence, his
hand clamped on my wrist over my long sleeve. I let him
lead me deeper into the forest. My heart thumped, eager to
find a secret place where we could strip our souls bare and
be with each other, without any threat of being found
hanging over our head.

"You've grown a little these past few moons," he said in
his beautiful, lilting voice.

"Gotten fat?" I asked with a coy look.

"No. More's the pity. I like a wee bit of meat on my
woman's bones."

I shook my head.

"I jest, Muriel. You're beautiful." His fingers brushed my
cheek.

Blushing, I arched away from his caress. I'd spent nights longing to feel his fingers on my skin, pressing the white flowers to my lips. But I'd been warned not to let a Berserker touch my skin. Fergus knew this as well. In the spell of the dark, quiet forest, and each other's presence, it was easy to forget the rules.

"Where are we going?"

His hand dropped to take hold of my wrist again. "Not much farther."

Finally, we reached a place where little light broke between the thick branches of the towering pines. A stream ran through the heart of a grove of ferns, and here Fergus stopped. Hands spanning my small waist, he lifted me and set me on a broad, flat stone splitting the rush of water, and stepped onto it with me. Before I lost my balance, he tugged me closer, holding me in his arms like we were a couple dancing at a midsummer fair.

"Fergus," I kept my eyes on the hard ridge of his muscle along the center of his chest. Lean and wiry, he was the smallest of his Berserker pack, but still two heads taller than me and much, much stronger. Stronger than any human in existence. "We shouldn't be together like this. It is forbidden."

"Muriel," the way he breathed my name sounded like a song, a prayer. "Look at me."

"I cannot," I kept my gaze averted. "Sabine says I must not look any members of the pack in the eye, or risk giving great offense."

"Any other warrior in the pack, aye. But not me. Never me. Look at me, wee one," He gave a command and tipped my chin up with a finger.

He had eyes of a storm far off over the ocean. When the

beast was upon him, they turned gold with an otherworldly light.

"I have things to say to ye, but I cannae say them yet. I haven't the right."

Now my cheeks were turning pink as heat poured through me in response to his touch. "Can you not say a few of them?"

"I would that I could. Some day, soon, I will. I'll tell ye all ye want to hear, and more." His promise sent warmth through my body. We had an ocean of difference between us--he was a Berserker of the Highland pack, and I was a captive and ward of their enemies; he was a werewolf, I was not--but in that moment we shared the same breath, the same heart.

Bowing his head, his forehead brushed mine, and his voice dropped to a deep rumble that spread tingles through me. "If I had my way, I'd show ye my thoughts as well as tell ye. Ye ken?"

I opened my mouth, and his head jerked.

"Do ye hear that, lass?"

"No."

"Your sister calls for ye." His tone held regret.

"I have to go." I whispered.

"I know."

I pulled free a ribbon from my dress Head bowed, I wrapped the green cloth around his bicep.

When I stepped away, he caught my hand, pulled me back. I leaned into him, my eyes closed, and his lips brushed mine.

I smiled the rest of the walk home.

FOR THE PAST TWO MOONS, I'd lived with Sabine in the great lodge her Alpha mates—Ragnvald and Maddox—had built for her. I wasn't surprised when I ran to the doors and they opened before me. A dark-haired warrior, clad only in leather breeches and the tattoos that covered his bare chest, waited inside.

"Muriel," he greeted me. "I'm glad you've returned. Your sister Sabine was worried you'd lost your way."

"I did for a moment," I told the bland truth; Fergus had led me off the path I knew. Wolves can smell a lie. "Where is my sister?"

"I was about to leave to look for you." My older sister stood over a great table spread with drying herbs. "Where is your cloak, Muriel?"

"I must have left it in the woods." Another half truth. Sabine frowned, and I dug in my pouch for the herb that had been my excuse to leave that morning. "Here is more feverfew. I followed the stream until I found a whole patch."

"Ah, so your path crossed a stream. No wonder Ragnvald couldn't track you."

"I would've eventually," Sabine's second mate, Ragnvald, entered the lodge behind me. "I just wanted to be sure I found her before the other wolf did."

"There was another wolf out there? Berserker?" Sabine asked.

"I smell him on you, Muriel. You must have come close to him."

I kept my head down and washed my hands. If I said anything, they'd scent a falsehood, and I could not give Fergus up.

"Too much coming and going between ours and the Highland Pack," Ragnvald muttered.

"Wolves come about to catch a peek of the women who

can mate with Berserkers. I know I would risk my life for a glimpse," Maddox said to Sabine, and he tugged a lock of her honey gold hair. She slapped at him, and he laughed.

Ragnvald stayed serious. " No more excursions out of the lodge alone," he told me.

"I understand," I said in a docile tone. Throughout my life I'd found I could quietly go my own way if I acted sweet and obedient.

Sabine was too stubborn to be submissive. "That's ridiculous," she frowned at Ragnvald, hands on her hips. "Spring is here. You cannot keep us cooped up."

"Just for a little while. Muriel will be leaving us, soon."

"I thought she was to stay with us, and Fleur with our sister Brenna." Part of the truce meant that the four of us were split evenly among the packs. Brenna was mated to the Highland pack's Alphas, Sabine to the Lowland Pack's. Soon, Fleur and I would have to take mates. No one had spoken of this to me, but I understood it all the same. We were still captives, even though we were treated with respect and care.

"We need to talk. Muriel, will you come here?" Ragnvald pointed to a place before him on the raised stone hearth. I went and sat with my hands in my lap. The very picture of meekness. The blond Alpha hadn't questioned me about the strange wolf he'd scented in the woods, and I was eager to keep from raising suspicion. One slip of my tongue, and my secret meeting would be revealed. I would get in trouble and might be disciplined, but Fergus would face the Berserker's wrath. His punishment might be death. The packs were very strict when it came to preserving their few potential mates.

I kept quiet as Ragnvald studied me.

"What's going on? What is this about?" Sabine set down

her mortar and pestle. Maddox hovered close to her, and she gave him a sharp look.

Ragnvald spoke directly to me. "As you know, all Berserkers met at the Gathering last week."

I nodded.

"Many things were decided there, so we might keep the peace between our packs. Two nights hence there will be a great competition. It will be a great contest of force, battle readiness and strength. Muriel, you watch the Games. Sabine and all the Alphas will all be there to oversee them, but you will be the guest of honor." He paused as if waiting for a response.

"I see," I said, even though I didn't. "I am happy to go where the treaty decrees. As always, my sisters and I are grateful for your hospitality and protection." Never mind that I was little more than a captive, my marriageability making me a useful pawn in the negotiations between the warring packs. If I kept quiet and remained obedient, I might be awarded more freedom. Perhaps I would see Fergus at these Games, and we could find another chance to slip away together to talk.

"The competition will decide who is the greatest Berserker among all the packs. There is a prize for the winner."

I thought I understood. "You wish me to attend these Games so I may award the prize?"

The two Alpha's exchanged glances. Ragnvald came to where I sat on the hearth and crouched in front of me.

"Muriel," he said gently, "you are the prize. You'll be given to the winner of the Games, and he will claim you as his mate."

For a moment the world spun. The fire burned too hot; my body flushed as if with fever. Ragnvald was still speaking, but I heard only a buzzing noise. Fergus' voice floated through my head, a whispered promise.

Sabine's sharp voice cut through the ringing in my ears.

"So she's to be given away like a trophy? Bound for life to a man who wins her in a contest? You could not give her a choice?"

"We would if we could. This is what was agreed after many nights of debate," Ragnvald explained. "The man who wins her will be the most powerful warrior in the pack. He will be worthy of a bride."

"Bride. Such pretty words for 'chattel'. You may as well be auctioning off a piece of meat," Sabine raged.

"Sabine," Maddox started.

Sabine whirled on him. "And if she refuses?"

"She cannot refuse. There is no escaping this. You knew this was coming. We all did," Ragnvald continued in his patient, level tone.

"She might disappear in the night. Stranger things have happened."

"We will be keeping close watch over her. Both packs have sent emissaries to guard her."

"We'll be watching you, also, Sabine. So you will not help her run."

Sabine snorted in disgust. Pushing away from the table, she kicked the chair so it clattered to the floor.

Maddox followed Sabine around the room, shadowing her as she paced in a temper.

"We leave tomorrow to reach the place where the Games will be held," Ragnvald told me.

"If she hates the warrior, can she refuse him?" Sabine asked.

Ragnvald hesitated.

"She can't can she? She could be given to the most awful,

brutish wolf in the pack, and can do nothing to escape him. Bound for life." Sabine spoke bitterly.

My tongue still lay heavy in my mouth, unable to move. My heart hurt. Had Fergus known what was decided for my fate? He must have had some idea. Perhaps his intent was to win the Games.

"Sabine," Maddox came behind his mate and slid his arms around her. She twisted to face him.

"It's not fair."

"It is as fair as we can make it."

"It's fair for every warrior in the pack. But not for her."

"Perhaps Muriel will decide that."

Sabine shook her head. With one final look at me, she ran from the room, Maddox following close behind. I heard them murmuring in their chambers at the far end of the lodge.

I still hadn't moved, though my hands were white where my fingers threaded tightly together.

"Muriel? Do you have anything to say?"

"My sister is very angry."

"She wishes her life was not directed by forces outside of her control. She is a force, like a great raging river. Sometimes she moves the rocks from her path. Other times, she must eddy around them. One day she will be powerful enough that nothing will stay in her way." Ragnvald's handsome face held a thoughtful look.

My sister had magic. A witch's prophecy foretold of a special race of women that carried a strain of magic to make them prime Berserker mates. So far, Sabine and Brenna have proved the prophecy true, and they expected Fleur and I to have the same ability. That was why they were so eager for us to marry within the pack.

"I always knew I must mate a Berserker," I ventured.

Ragnvald seemed to listen, he sat with a half smile, as if imagining his fiery mate. "I was hoping I would at least like whoever was chosen for my mate."

"Little sister, know that I would've made things easier for you, if I could. But the Games will satisfy the warriors in both packs. Otherwise there would be war between us." My sisters were happily mated to the Alphas of their respective packs. Sabine, for all her arguing loved Maddox and Ragnvald, and Brenna had borne her two Alpha mates children. War would threaten the love and new life, so fragile and dear to us all. "Already there are arguments and infighting over who will be awarded a Berserker bride. It's only a matter of time that a warrior challenges another for you and they fight until they destroy each other. We are doing all we can to avoid that."

"They are fighting...over me?"

A smile played around his mouth at my innocence. "You must understand what hope you give these men, Muriel. You and your sisters are the only women we've found to temper the curse. All the gold, all the bounty these warriors have fought for in the past century, nothing compares to the chance to win your hand in marriage. Believe me when I say these warriors will count it an honor to fight and bleed for you."

I couldn't think of what to say to that, so I stared at my hands, wishing I were braver, or stronger, or more clever tongued like Sabine.

"So whoever wins these Games I must take as a mate...like a husband?"

"In werewolf packs, a mate is more than a husband or a wife. The bond runs closer. This man, whoever he may be, will pledge himself to you and your care. He will be a devoted partner, protector, and leader, and will do everything within his power to keep you safe from all harm. Even die for you."

I swallowed hard. Berserkers lived like warriors, fierce mercenaries always ready for battle. I'd watched them training in their camps. They fought constantly, practicing, readying themselves for war. They were rough and brutal, given to violence at any moment. It was their nature.

I would be given to such a man.

"All right," I said finally. "I understand. Thank you."

"Of course, little sister. We will be watching over you, and will do all we can to help you." Ragnvald rose, and I knew he was eager to get to the bed chamber, and Sabine. The arguing had subsided, and given way to...other sounds. "Know this. Whatever wolf wins you, we can promise, he will treat you well. If he does not, he won't just answer to us. The Alphas would sit in judgment upon him, and he'd be lucky if we kill him ourselves, rather than give him over to the pack for them to tear him apart."

Later that night, I woke to harsh voices arguing. Sabine and her two mates slept on the far side of the lodge. Try as I might to keep a blanket muffling my ears, I often overheard their lovemaking.

Tonight there was more anger than love.

"You don't understand," Sabine was saying. "The twins are not like Brenna and me. They were coddled, sheltered. We kept them safe at all costs."

"We will do the same." Ragnvald sounded amused. "You think a Berserker cannot shield his mate from all harm? Muriel will be safer with a warrior from the pack than with any other creature on this island."

"I fear the Berserker rage more than any other force."

"You fear nothing, little witch," That was Maddox. "Much to our dismay. We wish you feared us. It would be easier to make you obey."

I imagined her swatting him away.

"You do your sister a disservice, thinking her so weak. She is stronger than you know."

"Her strength may break her. She will obey you, and at what cost? To spend the rest of her life shackled to some brute--"

"We will make sure she is well treated by whoever wins the Games. We need her to do her duty."

"Duty? She's a girl—"

"Who has the power to bring balance and stability to the pack. These warriors have gone so long without hope of living a normal life. Living as men. The Games gives them a chance to compete for what they desire above all," Maddox said.

"And when they see the strongest of them rewarded with a bride, they will accept his right over them," Ragnvald continued, "otherwise, I fear they will tear each other apart challenging for Muriel's hand. The Games will be violent, but not deadly."

"We hope."

"It is not right. Muriel should be able to choose. Perhaps we could wait, and see if she is like Brenna and me. Muriel may not have the magic that allows her to bond with a mate."

"You don't know that."

"She's never come into heat, as I did," Sabine insisted.

"You were a ripe fruit ready for us to pluck. Maddox stalked you for several moons, enjoying your scent."

"Tortured by it," Maddox muttered.

"My point is," Sabine sounded aggrieved. "Muriel may not be able to form a mating bond, as Brenna and I were able to. We should wait and see if her abilities grow."

A long pause, as if the Alphas were considering it.

"No," Ragnvald answered, finally. "There is no time."

"All will be well, Sabine."

"It's not fair," there was defeat in my sister's voice, "She should be mated to someone she can love."

"Perhaps, in time, she will come to love the one to whom she is given. After all, stranger things have happened. I recall a certain young woman who liked to stray from her home at night, who was taken by two Berserker warriors. She fell madly in love with them."

"You wish, wolf," Sabine said, but her tone was warm. A pause followed, filled with soft, passionate sounds I tried not to hear. When a low moan rose, I rolled over and clamped my blanket over my ears. Despite my worry, I smiled into the darkness.

"MURIEL, will you help me sort these herbs?" Sabine called me from my place staring into the fire. My own small bag was full and ready for our journey.

"I don't know what to bring," my sister fussed over her great table. Since our talk at the hearth, she'd been in a testy mood, as if she was going to be given to the Berserkers instead of me. After a heated argument, Sabine ordered her Alphas out of the lodge, and refused to let them back in. To my surprise, they obeyed, murmuring that they'd be back when it was time to leave for the Games.

The Games....I'd spent two days trying not to think of my fate, yet my thoughts swirled endlessly, reliving the conversation with Ragnvald and imagining what the Games would be like. Which warrior would win? In my dreams, I only saw Fergus' face, his red hair and sparkling eyes as he came to claim me as his prize...

"What are you thinking?" Sabine asked.

I shrugged and leaned on her table, toying with a few stems of dried angelica. Sabine covered my hand with hers.

"Muriel, my powers are still growing, but if you wish to leave now," she lowered her voice further, "I can call the witch Yseult. Her powers are greater than mine. She could help you escape."

I gave her a sad smile. "Where would I go?"

"Anywhere, far from here. The witch could hide you for a time."

For a moment, I toyed with idea of running away with Fergus. We could build a small cabin in a forgotten corner of the island, perhaps by the sea.

My foolish dream lived only a second. There was no corner of the earth where I could hide from these warriors. When they went to hunt, they tore great stags apart with their bare hands; if I ran, I'd be much easier prey. Besides, I would never put Fergus at harm. They'd take delight in destroying him.

No one could stop these Berserkers from taking what they wanted. And they wanted me.

I shook my head. "I cannot betray the truce. I'll be all right, Sabine. They will not mistreat me." I offered a fervent prayer to the goddess that this would be so. "I can do my duty. It is what the pack requires."

"Damn the pack! I wish the goddess would throw all the Berserkers in the sea."

"No, you don't. You'd miss them too much. At least two of them."

"I don't want you to sacrifice your life."

"You did. Would you change your fate?"

"No." Sabine gnawed her lip. "But, Muriel, remember that your fate is more than duty. You deserve to have a husband you love. I promised you once I would help you marry well, remember?"

"I remember," I couldn't keep the unhappiness out of my voice. I knew I was being selfish. My sisters Sabine and Brenna had been taken against their will to become Berserker mates, and had grown to love them. But was I strong enough to do the same?

2

The next day Berserker warriors came to escort me to the place where the Games would be held. These were men from the Highland pack. I looked for Fergus, but he was not among them. Ragnvald and Maddox were coming to represent the Lowland Pack, and wherever they went, their mate went with them, so Sabine was coming too. After the Games, she would take time to visit with Brenna and her new family, and relieve Fleur of some of the baby-watching duties.

I supposed I could help, too, if my new mate would allow it. My thoughts slid to Fergus. Did he like children? Would he raise them if I died birthing them? My sister had survived a difficult birth, but Sabine had told me Brenna had magic helping her. I had no magic. Would this make me an inferior mate? Would the Berserker who won me be disappointed and cast me aside? Would this threaten the peace?

My stomach churned and my foot caught my hem, making me stumble.

"Careful," one of the Berserkers held his hand out as if to break my fall, but did not touch me.

"Are you all right?" Sabine and her mates glanced back.

I hitched my dress up so it would not snag my boots. "Fine," I answered, and managed a smile. After a brief pause, Ragnvald gave the order and we marched on.

Walking in shadow between twin columns of the large warriors, I decided not to think about my life after the Games. I'd take this journey one step at a time.

We were headed to the Place of Stones, halfway between the Lowland and Highland Pack's home. The journey would've been quicker with horses, but the animals could not abide being near a Berserker. It would also be faster for the Berserkers to carry Sabine and I, as they have great strength and speed. But they could not because I was unmated and it would offend my future mate for the men to touch me, or so Ragnvald explained to me.

The day was fine and we made good time, so when Sabine requested we stop for lunch, her Alphas agreed. The three of them slipped off together leaving me standing stiffly with my honor guard. As the warriors handed out strips of meat, I drifted closer to a nearby stream. These men were on their best behavior, but I still kept a distance between myself and them while we waited for Sabine to finish with her lovers. I was used to the three of them disappearing like this, and did not fault them. Ragnvald and Maddox had nearly gone mad waiting for their true mate, the one who would balance the raging beast within and bring them peace. They needed connection with Sabine like food and air, and my sister was happy to comply. When she complained of their possessiveness, she did so with a smile.

My sisters were well matched with Berserkers, and happy. Perhaps I would be so lucky.

I found a rock near the pool and sat down, studying my reflection. Skin not dark or pale, but tan with faint freckles.

Long hair neither very blonde or very dark, but a dun brown. I wasn't short like Sabine, or tall like Brenna. There was nothing extraordinary about my looks or my person. Sabine had smarts and Brenna had courage, but I was lacking in both.

My hand dashed my reflection. At least one red-headed warrior had thought me beautiful. He was well built and strong, and he wanted me.

"Fergus," I whispered, touching my hair where I'd threaded the white flower. "If there was any magic in me, I would use it to find a way to bind us now."

"Does our company weary you so much that you'd speak to your own reflection?" A warrior with blond hair loomed over me. I'd noticed him before—he had fine looks but an unhandsome sneer on his face, and watched me in a way that made me uneasy.

"I know. Let us have some entertainment. A small tournament. Any man here can challenge me."

I rose and scooted away from the warrior, under the pretense of going to a berry bush to pick fruit for my lunch. If I was lucky, I would not attract any unwelcome attention.

The blond warrior faced the rest of the troop. I noted that none met his eyes—a sign that this bully was dominant in the pack. "Well, come on? Will no one challenge me? Winner gets a kiss from the prize."

At that, I stiffened. I might be no more than a prize to these men, but my kisses were mine to give. This warrior had no right to claim them.

"The winner will get nothing from me," I blurted. "I am not a bawd, earning my keep in your beds."

The blond warrior whirled and stalked back towards me, and I knew I'd made a mistake. He stalked closer, intent on tormenting me.

"No? Pity. It might be better for the pack if you were. Perhaps I will suggest it at the Gathering. We could pass you around and enjoy your charms. Why should one man claim what we all could share?"

I tensed as he bent over me, but stood my ground. "My fate has been decided."

"Such a shame. We could have had fun." He stepped closer, too close. Every instinct in me told me to run. I clenched my fists at my sides and forced myself not to look up at him, or strike out, goading him further.

I couldn't stop my sharp tongue. "I doubt I would enjoy it."

His voice dropped an octave lower, but the seductive purr only made my skin crawl. "It will be my pleasure to prove you wrong."

"Not unless you win the Games." Inwardly I shuddered at the thought of being shackled to such a bully.

When I started to move away, he caught my sleeve with a growl.

"Siebold," a deep voice rang out before I could lash out. "Take two wolves and patrol ahead."

The bully froze. "But--"

"Now." Even I felt the push of compulsion in the order. Berserkers were wolves who followed an Alpha, and a more dominant wolf had power over a weaker one. Whoever this Siebold was, he held sway over most of the warriors—but not all of them.

The blond left and my savior approached. Without thinking, I looked up...and looked up further. This man was enormous. Tall and broad, his heavily muscled form towered over me, enough to block out the sun. His legs were like tree trunks; his arms and shoulders stretching the leather jerkin he wore. He wasn't handsome—a scar slashed over his blunt features, and his grey stubble on his chin matched that of his shaved head—but he was striking, powerful. A force to be reckoned with.

At the last moment, I dropped my gaze.

"The rest of you, spread out. Form a perimeter," the giant ordered, and the rest of my escort obeyed. He remained, my sole protector.

Slowly, my body relaxed. I picked some fruit off the berry bush while the great warrior hovered at my side.

"You would do well to eat more than berries, little one." He offered me a strip of dried meat.

"Thank you, sir." I accepted, careful not to touch his fingers. I'd had little appetite lately, but I found it had returned. When I finished the meat, I unhooked a horn I wore at my belt, and filled it with water from the stream. The giant warrior stayed at my side, watching over me. I offered him the horn, first. He paused before he took it.

"Careful, Muriel. Sharing a drink with a warrior means more to him than it might to you." At my puzzled look, he explained. "Long ago, when a woman approached a man with a horn, it meant she had chosen him for the night. We remember some of these rules from the years when we were men."

"I'll take more care, sir." I didn't raise my eyes beyond the dip in the center of his chest. Pack rules didn't allow weaker members to look stronger ones in the eye. To do so was a challenge that could result in a fight to the death. In many packs, females that could not fight were punished for rising above their place. As a human female, I was weaker than any other, and this man was twice as tall and thrice as broad as me, the most powerful Berserker I'd ever seen. He could crush me with a single blow, yet I felt safe in his shadow, unlike with Siebold or most of the others.

"Look at me, little one," he rumbled. Nervous, I obeyed almost as soon as he gave the command. The scar gave his face a brutal look, but his grey eyes were kind.

"I thought..." I licked my lips and found my voice, "I was told I'm not supposed to look any wolf in the eye," I told him.

"It is wise to follow that rule carefully, but not with me. Never with me. My wolf doesn't see you as a threat."

I felt like he'd told me something important.

"Thank you, sir," I said, trying to be polite.

Grey eyes smiled.

"So brave. You did well, standing up to Siebold."

I pursed my lips. "He's a bully."

"He is. A dangerous one. You need to take care not to bait him, unless you're around me."

"I've never been good at holding my tongue."

"So I've heard. You were very brave when the Berserkers first took you, calling out to save your sister's life, making demands of the Lowland Pack even when you were their captive."

I blinked. "You heard of that?"

"Every wolf has heard of it." Reaching out, he tucked a strand of hair behind my ears. I jerked back, my heart tripping faster. This warrior dwarfed me in every way. His hands could span the width of my waist, but when his blunt fingers caught a handful of my long, brown tresses, his thumb stroked the shining lock of hair with surprising gentleness.

"My lord--" I protested, tugging the lock from his grip. Heat suffused my body as if he had touched my skin, and again my gaze fell to the chiseled muscles of his chest. Cheeks hot, I couldn't bear to look him in the eye.

"Wulfgar," he supplied, amusement in his tone.

"My lord Wulfgar, you should not touch me. It does dishonor to the man who will win my hand."

One side of his mouth creased in a half smile. "Is that so, little one? Then I had better win."

THE DAY of the Games dawned bright and sunny, but my stomach was a tempest.

Sabine helped me bathe the night before. She used oils to soften my skin and hair, and herbs to scent them. Once or twice she seemed about to speak to me of something beyond the 'what gown I was to wear', or 'what flowers she would weave in my hair', but I distracted her with idle chatter. I could not bear to hear her ask how I was, mostly because I wasn't sure I wouldn't break down and beg her to help me escape, even knowing how foolish it was.

I found myself seated with Sabine and the four Alphas on a giant rock that served as a dais overlooking the Games. Brenna and Fleur were not going to attend. Brenna stayed home with her twin boys, and Fleur was recovering from her most recent fever. I almost envied my twin's illness as I sat stiffly on display for the warriors competing for my hand. Grunts echoed up and down the field as Berserkers ran and clashed with one another in a skirmish whose rules I didn't understand.

Normally I'd enjoy being out in the sun on such a fine day, but I spent most of the morning staring at my folded hands, or at the banks of white wildflowers that lined the playing field. I still had the blossom Fergus had given me by the stream.

Ragnvald leaned close to me. "You may watch, Muriel. They compete for your honor."

Dutifully, I raised my gaze, but my eyes sought out only one form on the field. With his red hair, Fergus was easy to find--he wore the green ribbon I'd given him, tied around his bicep. He ran in man shape, rushing along with the others. The shortest and smallest of all the warriors, he looked like a boy among men.

My fingers clenched my skirts as I watched Fergus play ducking and weaving through warriors greater in size. For a moment he broke out of the pack, and caught a round pigskin they'd stitched into a ball. Warriors raced towards him, fencing him in as he threw the ball to another.

"Do ye know how this game is played?" One of the Alphas mated to my sister Brenna squatted next to me.

"No, my lord."

"Call me Daegan, wee sister," he grinned and I caught a glimpse of his elongated canines. Even in man form, Berserkers kept some lupine qualities, and moved with predatory grace.

"They compete now as two groups. The team who runs the ball through the goal there--" he pointed to a net stretched between a wooden frame, "gets a point."

The warriors now lined up across from each other. Maddox had left the dais to oversee this game. At his shout and piercing whistle, the two lines of Berserkers ran and smashed into each other.

Dropping my gaze, I winced at the brutal sounds.

"No blood is to be drawn at this point," Daegan continued. "Any player caught using an unfair advantage of weapon, tooth or claw will be disqualified."

I forced myself to watch again. Berserker brides could not be squeamish. Again and again the line of warriors formed, and the men clashed.

"How will a winner be chosen?" I asked, keeping an eye on a certain redhead fighting in the fray.

"This game will not decide your mate. The winning team will advance to the next contest and the losers will not. That is why they play with such ferocity."

On the field, one of the warriors slammed into the one who held the ball. As the man fell, the pigskin flew up in the air. Fergus sprang from the ground, seeming to fly as he reached out and caught it. When he landed, a group of the other team was waiting. They pounced and the red-head disappeared under a pile of warriors intent on crushing whoever held the ball. Dust flew; bodies disappeared in a knot of flailing limbs.

Gasping, I rose to my feet. Could Fergus, or any warrior, survive under the weight of so many Berserkers? My stomach churned but I could not look away.

Maddox ran at the pile, waving his hands and shouting. A great roar rang out, and blood sprayed in the dirt.

"Foul play," Daegan muttered. "Some of the warriors let the beast take them. I best help Maddox." Uncoiling from his crouch by my side, he leapt from the dais and ran to the dogpile that had turned into a brawl. Without hesitating, he and Maddox waded in, grabbing Berserkers and tossing them out of the fight. Some of the hulking warriors looked like monsters, their hands tipped with vicious claws, their muscles half covered with fur. The air crackled with magic and the hair on my arms stood on end.

"Muriel," Sabine laid her hand on my arm. "It's all right. The Alphas will sort it out. You don't have to watch if you don't want to."

"I must," I whispered. One of these men would be my husband. I'd thought so much of wedding Fergus, I didn't realize I'd be joined to a Berserker, a brute with the strength of a hundred men, and a rage that burned constantly. A rage only I could cool;or so the prophecy told.

The strange wind of magic died as the Alphas did their work quelling the beast's rage. On the field the knot of men unraveled, half of the players limping away. I relaxed when I saw Fergus' head bobbing with the rest. He ran to his side with the rest of his teammates; they threw their fists in the air and cheered.

"It's over," Ragnvald said. "The team that kept control of their beast, and the ball, won. Those that took beast form are disqualified."

Fergus' team lifted him on their shoulders. Their triumphant bellows shook the mountain.

I sagged in my seat in relief, and pressed a hand to my belly. Nerves kept me from eating much the past few days, but my stomach clenched. If I wasn't careful, I'd prove myself as weak as Fleur, my twin sister, and put the Games at risk. Sabine would insist the Alphas cancel the tournament for my illness. These Berserkers had waited so long for a chance at a bride. A delay would strain fragile peace between the packs.

No, I had to be strong. If my future husband could endure this brutal play, I could stand to watch.

My gut twisted further as the field cleared for the next game. Maddox left Daegan to oversee the players, and returned. Blood dripped down Maddox's tattooed chest, but I could not tell if it was his.

Sabine rose as if she would jump from the dais and rush to him.

"Stay, little witch," he called to her. "It is only a flesh wound." A single leap, and he stood on the dais beside her.

Ignoring the dust caked over his muscles, she pressed close to him to examine his wound.

"How do you like the contest, Muriel?" Maddox asked. My eyes caught the tear on his neck, the wound Sabine clucked over even as it healed rapidly.

The stench of blood and sweat and Berserker magic overwhelmed me and I had to turn my head away for a breath of clean air.

"Muriel?"

"I'm sorry," I choked out, and gestured to the sun. "The heat of the day is too much."

"Ragnvald, perhaps you could take Muriel for a walk out of the sun," Sabine suggested. "This is not the only field set for play."

"The others are practice fields," Maddox said. "The warriors wanted Muriel here, so she could see them fight."

"They will not miss her for a short time. I will stay and watch with Maddox so when the players look to the dais they will see a woman. Most of these warriors are so lust crazed, they cannot tell one woman from another, and certainly can't tell two sisters apart."

"They'd better," Maddox growled and pulled Sabine fully against him. "I will kill the wolf who touches my woman."

Sabine tsked but I could tell she was pleased.

"Come, little sister," Ragnvald beckoned. We walked from the field to the next, passing clumps of warriors waiting for their turn at the games. I covered my hair with a scarf and kept my eyes lowered so as not to draw attention, but it was no use.

As we passed the warriors turned and stared at me until my cheeks must have been bright red.

"The wolves are eager to compete for your hand." Ragnvald swept a hand to indicate I should precede him.

He hovered at my side, escorting me through the Berserkers.

There were many different types of games. Some ran obstacle courses in wolf form. Others climbed a sheer rock face with no rope or anything to soften their landing if they fell.

We came around the bend where the ground shook with a noise like thunder, to find warriors hefting boulders and heaving them as far as they could. They tossed and cheered like boys with rocks—only the rocks were two or three times their size.

At another station, two Berserkers wrestled on a large stone slab, their muscles bulging with the strain. Sweat ran in rivulets down their hardened chests.

"They try to push one another off the rock. Three times makes a winner."

As I watched, one of the warriors gnashed his teeth, threatening to bite his opponent. His claws grew and bit into the corded muscle of the man. Blood poured and the opponent roared.

"Why do you not cry 'halt'?" Ragnvald asked of a watching man. "Drawing blood is cheating. No assuming beast form."

"They're just practicing," the watcher answered with a shrug.

A few of the onlookers tried to catch my eye, so I stared hard at the fighting two instead.

I took a deep breath. How would Fergus even survive this?

"Any warrior turning into his beast will be automatically disqualified. Part of the games is proving their control. It would not do for us to reward a berserker with a mate, only to find he is too far gone to be saved."

I read the thinly veiled meaning: a Berserker who could not control his beast couldn't be trusted with a bride. If the beast broke free, I would not survive the wedding night.

"The final battle will be a one on one fight," Ragnvald continued. "Hand to hand combat. We will allow beast form then. Winner takes all."

Winner takes you, he meant. In all my eighteen years, I would never had guessed life would lead to this, a tournament of brutal games where I was the final prize. I'd expected to live my life in a village and take a farmer to marry. He would love me, but not covet me, like a dying man desperate for the cure.

With a hand hovering at my elbow, Ragnvald escorted me back to the dais. " Do not be surprised if your future mate takes the opportunity to put down his opponent. These Games count as a challenge for dominance." He may as well have been discussing the details of a hunt, but I understood the warning. The final contest would be a fight to the death.

I WATCHED and listened to the Alphas explain the tournaments as best they could, but could not keep my hands from clasping tighter in my lap. Fergus won a foot race, and managed to qualify in a ridiculous challenge that involved ripping up a sapling by its roots and throwing it like a spear at a target painted on a standing stone. He excelled at the group games, where his speed made him an asset to his team, and a target to the opposing one. I held my breath as he raced up and down a field, kicking a round ball. Berserkers tried to stop him, crashing into each other.

For a moment I had a wild hope that my redhead

warrior might beat out the rest and win, but disaster struck halfway through the team sport. A few of the opposing team made it a point to target Fergus and run him down. He ducked and dodged, and reached the goal, where, triumphant, he spiked the ball.

He didn't see his attacker coming, not until the man hit him like a boulder. Fergus' head and torso snapped back, the ball flew from his hands. The next thing I knew, I was on my feet. Fergus' attacker strode off, leaving the redhead crumpled on the ground.

"Foul play," muttered Ragnvald. "The goal was already gotten."

"They're giving him a penalty for it," Maddox said, "but that will not help the little wolf."

"Fergus, his name is Fergus," Daegan pointed to the fallen warrior. "It's all right, Muriel. He changes into wolf form to heal faster."

"Will he be all right?" The red and white feathered tail disappeared into the forest. I craned my head but couldn't see him slink away.

"He'll be fine. Berserkers can withstand most wounds."

"Will he come back?" I asked, even though I knew the answer.

"No," Maddox said after a pause. "He is disqualified."

I gave a stiff nod and settled back to watch the field, even though I barely saw the action. Sabine kept casting worried looks in my direction.

The field blurred once or twice, but I pretended it was the setting sun blinding me.

Finally, two warriors remained. They took their place on the field. I realized with a jolt that both were familiar—Siebold, the blond bully, and Wulfgar, the scarred warrior who'd stood watch over me.

"Who are these wolves?" Sabine asked. She'd moved her seat closer to me. Ragnvald sat beside her, and Maddox stood at the foot of the dais, ready to rush to oversee the games, if needed.

"The scarred hulk is called Wulfgar. He came from Norway with the rest of the pack," Ragnvald said.

"I know Wulfgar. He is a good warrior," Maddox said. "Possibly the greatest fighter in the pack. They call him 'The Enforcer.'"

"Why?" Sabine asked, her eyes still fixed on the warrior with the shaved head.

"Because when the Highland Alphas need to bring order to the pack, they call on him. He's good at killing wolves."

"The only thing that can kill a Berserker is another Berserker," Ragnvald muttered.

"I see," Sabine said sharply, after glancing at me. "And who is the other?"

"The other's name is Siebold. He..." Maddox grimaced, shook his head.

Ragnvald spoke instead, "Pray that Wulfgar wins."

I sent my prayers to the goddess. Daegan raised a red cloth and let it fall—the signal for the final tournament to begin. Time slowed and my heartbeat thudded hard in my chest as the two opponents circled each other. Magic rippled the air, and the warriors were men no longer, but great beasts, hulking with furred limbs and large paws tipped with ferocious claws.

The monsters ripped at each other. I knew not which was which. A claw caught one of the beast's shoulders, slicing through flesh. Blood sprayed on the ground and I flinched. The warriors howled.

"First blood, Siebold," Maddox said.

After that I didn't bother looking any more. Let them

think I was too weak and squeamish to look. I'd bound wounds before, and helped Sabine set a broken bone but I could not stand the senseless violence of this final Game. All this gore just to win my hand.

If peace hadn't hung in the balance, I would've stood and left. As it was, I took deep steadying breaths, and told my flopping stomach to behave.

I startled when a tall warrior crouched before me. Samuel, a Viking of old, Alpha of the Highland Pack, and one of my sister Brenna's consorts. He leaned close, as if to offer me a horn of water.

"You don't have to do this," he said. He looked unhappy.

At my side, Sabine gripped my arm harder.

"What do you mean?" she asked for me.

"When the Games are over, we can call for a new Gathering. The winner will feel cheated, but they will come around."

I'd heard that Brenna's mate Samuel had moments of tenderheartedness.

"Will that mean war?" I asked. My voice sounded hoarse. "Among the packs?"

He hesitated. "These men mean well. They've fought their beast for so long, but the presence of you and your sisters has brought hope. It may be enough to tide them over until we find more women who can mate with them. Brenna has argued with me these past few weeks, telling me there are better ways to choose a mate for you."

I stared at him, wondering why he waited until now, with the sounds of the final tournament ringing out under a sunset sky, to give me a choice. To absolve him of his guilt? What would happen if I agreed? Another Gathering, more strain on these brave warrior's patience, their tenuous hold on their feral nature? At the worst, a few might lose control, and then what? A great fight? People would die. Fergus could die.

"Did you hear him, Muriel? You don't have to take the winner as your mate against your will," Sabine encouraged.

Somehow I found the strength to speak. "Yes, I do. You know I do."

"Muriel..." Sabine started, and I cut her off.

"No, sister. I will do my duty, if not for the good of the pack, then for you and Brenna, and your future children." Peace must be kept, at any price. Even at the cost of my heart.

My sister fell silent.

Samuel regarded me solemnly. Sabine had told me about him, that the Viking was the wisest of the Berserkers, a leader and a scholar, as well as a deadly fighter. I felt I would shatter under his stare.

Finally, he nodded and offered me the horn, which I took and drank to slake my thirst. It wasn't water, but mead and it burned all the way down.

Another roar from the crowd. I tried not to hear the desperate grunts and growls and sick, wet sound of teeth and claws ripping flesh.

I clutched the horn, risking only one more glance at the field. Billows of dust obscured the two grappling forms. The flowers would all be gone, I noted, crushed under the battle. Would grass ever grow again where the ground was soaked with blood?

A great roar and a clang of an ax on blade. My fingers were white knuckled on the horn.

"We have a winner," Daegan announced. "Come forth warrior, and claim your prize."

Out of the corner of my eye, I saw Sabine rise. Her

mouth opened, and I knew she was going to try to call a halt to the Games on my behalf. Everything would be lost.

I shot to my feet before she could say anything.

"To the victor go the spoils," I shouted, holding the horn high. To my surprise, the Berserker warriors took up my proclamation.

Goosebumps ran up and down my arms as they responded in eerie unison. "To the victor go the spoils."

Ignoring the shivers in my body brought on by a strange wind, I strode for the dais steps, and would've tumbled off if Maddox wasn't there to help me to the ground. Once there, I almost lost my nerve, but one glance at the Alphas standing on the dais and I knew I could not return to their protection. Somehow I'd invoked pack magic, and now I was caught in a ritual. I dared not break the spell, and risk stripping the last bit of ceremony from these violent men.

With the wind at my back, I let my feet carry me onto the field. The throng of warriors parted for me to pass. Some were in beast form, I was sure, though I dared not look closely as I passed. The stench of blood hung in the air.

Between the ranks of Berserker warriors, I saw a crumpled shape on the ground, obscured by the dust of the fight. As I grew closer, I still couldn't recognize the misshapen mess of skin, wounds and fur. One giant hand extended from the bloody bundle, with three long and vicious claws. The fourth was broken.

I swallowed down bile at the sight, and the faint wheezing sound. The warrior was not dead, but almost. As Ragnvald predicted, defeat came at a high cost.

Then I saw the victor.

Wulfgar stood with head bowed and chest heaving. His opponent had ripped a bloody gash from shoulder to opposite hip, tearing the muscle. The slash mark matched the old scar marring his blunt features. His short hair was caked with dirt and sweat. Yet he was standing.

Behind me, Maddox announced, "I declare Wulfgar the rightful winner of the games." Dust rose again as the warriors stomped their feet and cheered. I ignored them all.

Clutching the horn like a talisman of protection, I walked straight up to the giant warrior. Sweat slicked his features and his great muscles.

"Your prize, my lord." My hands shook a little as I raised the horn, but my voice sounded sure.

This time, Wulfgar did not hesitate to take what I offered. Wrapping one large hand over my own, he lifted the horn, I stretched to tip toe and drank. He never took his eyes from mine.

When the horn was drained the triumphant roar of the Berserkers finally reached my ears and I swayed. He touched my arm and steadied me.

"My lady."

His hand settled at my nape, and caressed it gently. His rough fingers slid over my smooth skin with gentle reverence, and under my numbed emotions I felt a flicker of life.

If the Alphas gave speeches, I did not hear them. I barely saw the faces of the warriors who faced us, or heard their cries. All the triumph and defeat drained away to silence in the protective shadow of the giant warrior who was now my mate.

With a hand at my waist, he led me away, and the warriors parted before him. I dared not look left or right until we reached the edge of the field, and then I erred. I peered into the forest and saw the ripple in the underbrush where a familiar red wolf slipped away.

My boot caught the train of my fine gown, and I stumbled.

Without pause, Wulfgar caught me up in his mighty arms. Curled against his powerful chest, I clutched at one great arm and forced myself not to tremble as I caught sight of his stern countenance. Had I already displeased him? He probably didn't want me looking at other wolves. I waited, but he didn't speak. Cradling me gently, he didn't break his stride as he plunged into the darkness between the trees.

3

We reached a cabin in the woods just as the last light of day faded. Torches tipped with pitch burned outside its doors. Wulfgar carried me over the doorstep and only then set me down on the rough hewn boards that made the floor.

In addition to the torches outside, the inside of the dwelling had been made ready for us. The hearth fire burned with a pungent smoke and beside it sat skins of wine and a pot filled with stew. I even saw a kit of healing herbs I could use to clean Wulfgar's wounds.

A large portion of the cabin was taken up by a massive bed. The sight of the soft mattress heaped high with pelts made me pause.

I swayed a little.

"Muriel," the giant warrior steadied me.

I glanced down and realized the fine dress I wore was stained with gore. In the close space, Wulfgar reeked.

"We need to clean that wound," my hands fluttered over the gash in his muscled chest. "Carrying me made the tear worse."

"It was worth it," he said quietly, and heat suffused me.

"I, uh, can make a poultice...I just need water."

Wulfgar picked up a bucket by the door. "I'll return in a moment."

There seemed to be more air in the cabin when the great warrior left. It was bad enough that the bed took up most of the space in the single room. There was no other place to sit, not even near the fire. Once Wulfgar was clean and bandaged, he could very well strip me down and take me on the pelts. Would he go slowly and make sure I enjoyed it? Or fast, rutting me like an animal?

Stop it, I scolded myself. Don't think too far ahead.

Stupid, that I hadn't realized what being mated to a Berserker meant. At least I'd been given to Wulfgar and not Siebold.

It could've been Fergus, I thought, and pain sliced my heart. He was young and sweet and I could've loved him forever, but I couldn't allow myself to think on it. Right now I had to learn to love this brutal warrior. Some day I'd allow myself to grieve Fergus and what we might have had.

A shadow moved to my left and I jumped. Wulfgar moved quietly for a such a large warrior.

"My lady," he said and touched my gown, now stiff with blood.

Water beaded on his huge arms, and I realized he'd washed in the stream. He lifted the bucket.

"I can fetch more water, if you wish to bathe. Though I fear your gown is too stained to save."

"Tis nothing."

"Please, Muriel. The scent of blood calls the beast."

At that, I stripped off my overdress and threw it out the door. My shift was made of plain, undyed linen, but it was enough to cover my form. Wulfgar's eyes followed me as if I was clothed in the finest, form fitting silk, but it was better than him losing control.

I faced the fire for a moment to regain a shaky grasp of my nerves. "I will see to your wound, if you will sit."

My heart pounded faster when I heard him settle onto the bed.

Somehow I made it across the cabin to stand before him. As I worked, I kept my eyes on his broad chest, studying the weals and scars from a lifetime of battles and brawls. His whole life lay under my fingers, mapped on the firm muscle. The Berserkers were created by a witch's curse long ago. Who was this man? What old pain lay beneath the scars and lines on his face?

The gash ran deep over his heart, but the shallower ends were already closing. I ran fingers coated with healing salve over the worst places. At one point I had to work out a piece of Siebold's claw, still stuck in Wulfgar's flesh. The warrior didn't even flinch at that. Yet when I stroked the ridge of an old scar, lower on his abdomen, he shivered and his hips jerked once.

I stopped my examination at once.

"Forgive me, little one," he said in a harsh voice. "It has been a long time, and the beast has been close to the surface all day."

His golden eyes eyes pinned me. "What should I do?" I whispered

"Be still a moment." He bent closer, his breath stirring my hair. I stood frozen like prey hoping a predator will pass it by. After a moment, he sat back with a sigh. "It's all right. Please continue."

"If you'll stand, I can tie the bandage." Relief poured through me when he moved away, off the bed.

I had a nasty thought. Would Wulfgar expect me to

already know how to please a man? My sisters had given me instruction, some straightforward and some more confusing. What if my new mate was disappointed in me?

I almost jumped when he spoke. "You don't need to fear me."

"Why not?" I asked, head bent to my work. I kept my tone light. "The rest of the pack does. Or should, after they watched you beat Siebold into a pulp."

As I reached for the herbs, he caught my wrist. "The Games were necessary. And fair. Siebold knew what he was getting into."

"Siebold is a bully." When Fergus had been tackled, the blond had stood on the sidelines, laughing.

"He is."

"Then he deserved what he got."

He let me finish tending his wound in silence. When I was done packing the poultice, he stood and rolled his shoulders, testing the binding.

"Thank you, little one."

I bent to pack the unused bandages away. "It would've healed without my herbs. The gash was already closing."

"The magic that makes us what we are allows us to heal much faster, but my powers were focused on fighting today. And I believe that Siebold used poison."

"Poison?" I looked at the claw with horror.

He shrugged. "Not a deadly one, but some sort of irritant he could dip his claw in. Not exactly against the rules, but it will delay healing."

My hatred of the blond bully increased, as did my rapport with this blunt faced warrior. "That's horrible. I wish you had had a more honorable opponent."

"I don't," he said. "If Siebold had been honorable, I wouldn't have taken so much joy in his defeat."

I recalled the bloody pulp on the field, and any connection I'd felt with my new mate vanished.

Wulfgar cleared his throat. "And anyway, your ministrations are always welcome. It has been a long time since a woman took care of me."

I nodded, and scuttled to the hearth to put distance between us. My foot hit a stew pot and the top clattered off, filling the cabin with a rich, meaty smell. Whoever had prepared the cabin for us had left us a meal. "There's food, if you wish to eat."

My stomach in knots, I barely touched my meal, while he demolished two platefuls. Other than crossing the room to serve him, I remained by the hearth as far away from him and the bed as I could be.

When at last he finished, I took a deep breath. It was time to act, before I lost my nerve.

I stood, drew the shift over my head, and let it fall to the floor. Standing with my naked form bathed only in firelight, my chin went up, but I couldn't quite keep my voice from breaking, "If it pleases you, I'm ready, my lord."

At first, Wulfgar did nothing at all. When he finally stood up, I flinched, and he paused again. With a slow measured tread that reminded me of a hunter's, he advanced.

He touched my face, and I realized I was crying.

"Oh," I took a step back and ducked my head to dash the few tears away. "I'm sorry. I'm a silly girl. It's just been a long day...and I'm not very brave."

Seating himself on the bed, he pulled me between his legs. I relaxed into his heat, even though I still quivered.

"I think that it has been a long day, and the best thing for us is sleep."

My shoulders drooped. Already I had failed him. I

started to dissent and he cut me off. "I need to rest as much as you."

"Forgive me--"

"I don't need your apology," he said mildly. "And while I am grateful for your...willingness, I think it will be better for us to take things at a slower pace. We have a lifetime together, after all."

"Al-all right."

"Promise me one thing." His finger tipped up my chin. "You will not think of yourself as a coward. It takes a lot of courage to disrobe in front of a stranger, a warrior you just saw lay waste to his opponents. Opponents who aren't even enemies, but fellow packmates who did nothing wrong beyond competing for your hand in marriage."

I gulped. Wulfgar had left Siebold as little more than a blood-soaked bag of skin and bones. "They will heal, though, right?"

"They will. You need not worry about them. We all would have done anything we had to, to win you." He let his head fall then, resting his forehead against mine.

His fingers tightened on my arm. I stayed very quiet, listening to him breathe.

When he raised his head, his eyes were bright gold. "It would be wise if you don't speak of the other men in the pack again. For tonight at least. My beast is excited at winning the battle, and ready to finish the hunt."

I swallowed hard. I didn't ask who was the prey.

"I will never harm you, and I swear I will do my best to be gentle, but you are mine now, Muriel. And I will never let you go."

∼

LATE THAT NIGHT, I lay beside my new husband, with my tears leaking onto the pelts. Over and over I saw Fergus fall. At least he had not been killed, I told myself.

Beside me Wulfgar slept like the dead. Wiping my wet cheeks, I rose and went to the fire. I'd woven the little flower Fergus had given me into a band I wore around my wrist. I broke the band and fed it to the fire. I couldn't go back to the past, only forward.

"Goodbye Fergus," I whispered, and returned to bed with my new husband, who didn't stir.

AT SOME POINT in the night, Wulfgar left the bed, for I woke a few times and he was no longer lying next to me. The fire in the hearth remained well tended, and in the lovely warmth, I fell back asleep.

I dreamed of a fire rising and consuming me in the bed, until I lay in the center of the blaze but my skin did not burn. The flames became hands that stroked my bare flesh and slid over my stomach to part my legs. Fingers caressed my hip and massaged my legs and buttocks.

The fire turned into coarse marsh grass rubbing against my back

My eyes fluttered open. There was a man behind me, running his hands over my bare flesh, stirring up the fire within.

Since I had met Fergus, I'd often imagined a man holding and touching me just like this. I had not forgotten the events of yesterday, I knew this was not Fergus, but still, I could pretend...

Closing my eyes again, I let the fingers drive my excitement higher. My newfound lover knew just how to touch me, how to explore soft curves of my body and circle ever closer to my most sensitive areas, keeping my breath on edge.

"Please," I sighed when the callused fingers delved between my legs, stroking the thin skin of my thighs. I shifted to my back, and my legs fell open in invitation.

"Is this what ye want, wee one?" A rough voice, barely recognizable as a man's. The Berserker beast was close to taking control, but I didn't care.

Lips touched the back of my neck and slid to my shoulder. I sucked in a breath as canines lightly pricked my skin. The beast wanted to bite, to mark me. In that moment I was willing to bleed, if only the hand would not stop its movement between my legs.

Pressing into the firm chest at my back, I parted my legs further and bent one into the air. The thumb ran along my lower lips, sending a shiver through me. My whole core was swollen and ready, pulsing. Fingers dipped into my wet heat and spread my honey over the petals of my sex. My hips jerked. A second arm snaked around my waist, drawing me flush against the long, hard body.

If I closed my eyes, I could pretend I was with Fergus, and not any other.

The hand between my leg started working, palm rubbing against the top of my sex sending little sparks shooting through me. My hips worked, rocking in rhythm. Warmth rose in me, building pressure ready to break and rush through me.

"Yes," I sighed.

Teeth scraped my sensitive shoulder. Somehow the threat of pain blended with the advent of pleasure and pushed me closer to the edge.

A low moan rang in my ears, vibrating from deep within

my chest. My body was not my own; it belonged to the hand relentlessly moving between my legs.

I grabbed the wrist with one hand, but my lover was too strong. Canines pricked my flesh just as my orgasm washed over me.

My gasping cry faded as the man behind me pressed his lips to my nape. I rolled to my back, Wulfgar's name on my lips. My voice died as Fergus smiled down at me.

"Good day, Muriel," he said.

"How…" my voice was still clogged with sleep and my tongue slow to find itself after such pleasure. I glanced at the door.

"Thought I'd sneak in and spend the morning with ye."

I pushed up, icy fear pouring through me, driving out any warmth. "Fergus, you cannot be here." I pushed at his chest and he caught my hand and kissed it.

"Ye wish me to leave?"

My eyes were only for the door. "Please. You must go. You must run. This is wrong, so wrong."

"Muriel—"

Wrenching my arm away, I staggered naked out of bed. One night, and I'd already betrayed Wulfgar. What would my given mate say when he returned and found the little red wolf in his new mates bed? Wulfgar had left Siebold a bloody mess on the field.

If he caught Fergus, the smaller redhead would not survive.

"Sweetling, calm yourself."

I backed away on bare feet, "You need to go. I'm sorry. I belong to another now. I will not break my vows. The peace is at stake."

The door behind me creaked open. Fergus' gaze went to

the the cabin floorboards which shook a little as Wulfgar entered.

"Muriel."

"My lord," I whirled. "I'm sorry." My stomach clenched like a giant's fist squeezed it. Eyes stinging, I pleaded as best I could. "Please, please do not hurt him."

"What is going on?" Wulfgar looked from me to the bed, Fergus.

"It was my fault,." I could barely whisper. "I led him on, made him believe..."

Wulfgar didn't speak; his face was stone. The creaking behind me told me Fergus was off the bed, coming towards me.

His hands caught my hips and started to draw me aside. "Muriel, it's all right."

Wulfgar finally spoke. "You lay with her?"

"Please," I threw myself between Fergus and the giant warrior. "Please have mercy. It was my fault. He is the first Berserker I knew and I fell in love. It was silly, stupid. I didn't know I was going to be a prize in the Games."

For a tense moment Wulfgar didn't say anything. I had a wild thought of me falling to my knees to beg, and Wulfgar leaping over me and gutting Fergus as he did Siebold. It didn't matter what I did. The giant warrior could easily sweep me aside to kill his rival.

Wulfgar rumbled. "You are more than just a prize, Muriel. Your opinion matters."

I opened my mouth, then closed it because I didn't know what to say to that.

"Do you care for him then?" Wulfgar asked me, jerking his head towards Fergus.

'I...yes. I always will. But I am your mate now. I know

that. I will do my duty and be true to you. I was weak. Please don't kill him."

Fergus' breath stirred my hair. "It's all right, Muriel." If I wasn't so worried, I'd say he sounded amused. "He won't kill me."

I tried to tell him to run, to save himself, but the words caught in my throat as he set me gently out of the way and approached Wulfgar.

"Indeed," Wulfgar said with a touch of amusement. "I won't kill you, but you won't live long if you don't remember to watch her back around Siebold and his cronies." His hand flung out to cuff Fergus, but the young wolf ducked. I gasped, but when Fergus righted himself he was smiling.

"What did I tell you about baiting that blond bully?" Wulfgar grumbled. "Good thing you're quick as a cowardly rabbit."

"Nice to see ye too, ye cranky old wolf. I was worried. Did no one teach ye to duck a blow before ye parry? Good thing your head is made of granite, otherwise ye wouldn't have survived. " Fergus said, and when Wulfgar growled and swatted at him, he danced lightly out of the way.

My mouth hung open as I watched them pretend to spar.

"Enough," Wulfgar said, and shoved Fergus away. "Go stoke up the fire." Before I could blink the giant warrior had crossed the room, and wrapped me in a pelt. With his massive form, I kept forgetting how swiftly he could move.

"We have a mate now," he said, tucking the pelt around me with tender hands, and tsking when he saw my bare feet on the cold floor. Only then did I realize I'd been shivering, and my breath hung like smoke on the bitter air. Lifting me easily, Wulfgar carried me back to the bed. "We need to take better care of you."

"Someone ought to explain how Berserker bonds work," Fergus gave Wulfgar a pointed look.

"What's going on?" I looked from one to the other.

"You thought I would kill him for claiming my bride before me?" Wulfgar asked.

I nodded, as I could barely speak.

"Any other wolf I would. But Fergus and I share a bond, much like your sisters' Alpha mates." Wulfgar explained. "We share everything."

"Everything," Fergus called. When I looked at him he waggled his eyebrows at me.

"Though," Wulfgar frowned at the younger wolf. "I should snap his neck for your first pleasure was mine to claim."

I gasped.

"He's joking, Muriel," Fergus said, and faced Wulfgar. "Not my fault ye left the bed. "

"She needed sleep."

"She woke easily enough for me," Fergus smirked.

Wulfgar growled and started to move, automatically I caught his burly arms. My hands were fragile as flower petals on a great corded trunk of a tree, but I made him still.

"You plead for his life?" Wulfgar half frowned, and I quavered even though I knew he was mocking me.

"Sweetness, he was teasing me." Fergus came to the bed, still wearing an amused look. "Are ye still frightened?"

"I didn't...I don't know." A knot in my chest unraveled, and unleashed my tears.

Wulfgar let me go and Fergus took his place. "It's all right, Muriel," he crooned. "Cry it out."

Clinging to him, I did. My sobs loosed all the tight emotions I'd locked up at the Games, the pressure that had weighed upon me ever since Ragnvald told me of my role in them.

The whole time, Fergus cradled me, whispering comforting things. Wulfgar also hovered, concern on his scarred face.

Finally, I shrank back and wiped my face. I should not be crying. Neither of my sisters would show such weakness. I was a Berserker bride now.

I crossed my arms over my chest, where the pelt had slipped, exposing my breasts. Wulfgar noticed my embarrassment and handed me my shift.

Fergus gave a mock grimace. "What's that for? We'll be helping her out of it soon enough."

"That depends on our mate," Wulfgar said. "It may take her a day or two to grow comfortable with us."

"Ye aren't frightened of us, are ye, Muriel?"

"No." I ventured a smile.

"Ye love me," he grinned with satisfaction. "Ye cannae deny it. I heard ye."

I blushed. "I thought you were going to die."

"He threatens to snap my neck once a day, but it's only in jest. Warrior brothers share a bond closer than the rest of the pack."

"Only a crazed wolf would attack his brother," Wulfgar added. "And then only after the bond is severed."

"Such lovely talk for a wedding morn." Fergus clucked. His jesting tone lightened my spirits, as did the added protection of my shift held against my naked chest.

I didn't miss the excitement in both warriors faces, or the way their gaze flicked over my barely covered curves. "When did you arrive?"

"I came here last night, but ye were both sleeping. I

stood guard for a time, but once Wulfgar left the bed, I couldnae resist taking his place."

"What time is it?"

"Past noon. Ye slept away half the day. Well, slept, and did other things."

"You took your time joining us, Fergus," Wulfgar grunted.

"I thought I'd spend some time in the pack, to learn how Siebold is planning to steal Muriel from ye."

I raised my head in alarm, but neither warrior seemed surprised.

"Do you think he will come soon to seek vengeance?" Wulfgar asked.

"He's still recovering, but he has friends in the pack." Fergus shrugged.

"He's up to something," Wulfgar shook his head.

"If he thought to challenge ye for your high place in the pack, the beating ye gave him knocked that thought right out of his head." Fergus sounded cheerful for such a blood-thirsty subject.

As usual, Wulfgar noticed my uneasiness at the violent talk. "Fergus," he chastened in a quiet voice, but his eyes were on me.

"I'm fine," I bowed my head, letting my hair fall over my face. "The pack is different from what I'm used to."

"A new world. And you're a brave one to enter it."

I didn't have a choice, but I didn't mention that.

"So," I looked from one warrior to the other, "you are both my mates?"

"The Alphas have a theory that without available mates we formed warrior bonds to support us through the centuries. Now that we have found you, we can claim you together. Our bond means we can share without quarreling."

"That means we'll share ye," Fergus winked at me, and I gulped. I was looking forward to seeing the Highlander naked again, this time without the loin cloth...but two men? At the same time? I touched my cheeks, wondering if they burned scarlet through the curtain of my hair.

"Fergus, can you go fetch water?" Wulfgar growled, and threw a bucket at his head. While the younger warrior loped off, Wulfgar rose and checked the fire. I took the moment of privacy to dress, and thanked my scarred mate when he tossed me my boots.

He stayed across the room from me, giving me space and moving with none of the speed that took my breath away.

"Will you check my cuts?"

I crossed to him and undid the bandages. The wounds were healing nicely, the least of them gone completely, faded into barely visible red marks. I cleaned and packed the worst cuts so they would not fester before wrapping them again. In this, at least, I was competent. I'd learned from Sabine, and she was always quick with criticism when I did something wrong.

As I finished I realized I'd spent a number of minutes at my giant mate's side, silent and totally comfortable. My gaze jerked up to his and when he smiled at me, I flushed.

"You must think me so stupid," I muttered.

"Never," he murmured, catching my arm and guiding me before him. "I'm not fond of hearing you call yourself 'stupid.' To me and the pack, you seem to be the finest of women."

"A prize to be won," I tried to joke, and couldn't quite.

"You are more than chattel. You are a woman, with a heart. I promise to handle it with care." He frowned.

"Muriel, how much did your sisters explain to you of being mated to a Berserker?"

"They told me how I might lay with a man. They told me how I might conceive. They mentioned their two mates shared them, but...." I trailed off, trying to remember the advice Sabine had given me, but all I could recall was the soft expression on her face when she described the mating bond, followed by a matter of fact explanation about men's cocks and women's heat. At some point, she remembered a time Maddox and Ragnvald annoyed her, and her teaching turned into a furious rant about 'making my voice heard and refusing to yield,' which turned into another rant about the unfairness of the Games. She'd then stormed out to 'find those monsters and tell them this won't stand.' She returned a few hours later, hair mussed and face flushed, but features serene.

All in all, it had been a confusing session, and now, faced with this powerful warrior, any useful advice flew out of my mind. "I-I wish I knew more."

"No matter." He tucked the hair back away from my face. "When the time comes, it will be our honor to teach you."

The door banged open with Fergus' arrival. "Here's your water. And the pack left food outside. A whole feast. They dinnae expect us to leave for some time." Fergus waggled his brows and I blushed all over again.

The two warriors bade me stay inside while they brought in a small table laden with oatcakes, roast boar, fowl and root vegetables cooked in a fig sauce. My stomach growled.

"Let us eat, then," Wulfgar gestured as soon as Fergus had brought in two chairs. I followed the warriors to the table, a hand on my stomach to stop its slight churning.

Wulfgar wanted to eat, so I would eat, so tonight I could do my best to please both my mates.

The two men sat but the lack of a third chair brought me up short.

"Sit here, Muriel," Fergus patted his knee.

Giving up hope that my cheeks would ever be anything but bright red for the rest of the day, I perched on his knee.

"It's alright, sweetheart," he murmured. His strong arms cradling me made my embarrassment worth it. "This week is for ye to learn about your husbands and how to please us. By the end ye will be used to all our attention, even welcome it."

"I am glad for your attention," I said. My body tingled as I lay my arm around his neck to steady myself.

"Good. One day ye will know that before ye sit down to dine with us, ye must be as naked as we are clothed."

"What..." I glanced at Wulfgar for confirmation. The big wolf was grinning but he didn't deny it.

"Strip, Muriel," Fergus said firmly.

My mouth dropped open. "What if someone comes in?"

"No one will disturb us. If they do, trust your mates to keep ye safe."

I frowned, but it seemed little to indulge him. After all, I was only wearing a shift. Fergus helped me pull it over my head.

"In the future, whenever ye hesitate to obey, ye will be punished."

"Punished?"

He nodded gravely, an excited light in his eye.

Wulfgar spoke up. "Nothing too harsh, and nothing that permanently harms you. But it is a great pleasure for a wolf to bring his mate to heel."

They both seemed so happy, I wasn't sure if they were joking. I decided to wait and ask Fergus later, in private.

Nodding, I pulled off my dress and shift, and reseated myself on Fergus' knee. The rest of the meal we amused ourselves. Fergus treated me as if I was fully clothed though the men's hot gaze on my bare form kept me warmer than the hearth fire. After placing a horn to my lips for me to drink, Fergus fed me choice bits from his own fingers and wouldn't let me touch any food.

After a few gulps of mead, I giggled and ate as if this was a clever game.

Fergus held a plum for me to bite, and its juice escaped down my chin, dripping onto my chest. He caught my hand before I could swipe at it with my fingers, and bent his head to lap it from my skin instead. His tongue chased a bead of sweet liquid almost to the cleft between my breasts. My head lolled back as his beard scraped my tender skin, sending strange but pleasant shivers through me. When he raised his head, droplets of plum juice clung to his lips and coarse red stubble. He kissed me and I found a new way to eat my favorite fruit.

When our mouths parted, I realized the hard bulge under my leg was growing larger.

Fergus really was the most handsome man I'd ever seen. I stroked his reddish sandy hair and he trailed his fingers up and down my bare back, pressing a kiss to my shoulder. I lapped at his fingers as he popped more food into my mouth, laughing when he kissed my ear and tickled it with his beard.

"Enough," I said. "I am full." I reached for the drinking horn instead, and Wulfgar made a dissenting noise. Fergus set it away.

"No more of that, sweet one."

"I'm always sweet. Never saucy. I always do as I'm told," I pouted. The mead I'd drunk made the room swim a little.

"Ye do?" Fergus murmured. "Then I shall have to give ye many orders. Give me a kiss, Muriel."

He didn't have to tell me twice. After what seemed like hours in his lap, teased by his fingers and clever lips, I only wanted more. I pressed my mouth to his, tasting the plum and mead.

I licked my lips. "Sweet. And tart."

His hand tightened in my hair and he used it to tilt my head, controlling the kiss. When he broke away, his breath caressed my face.

"My warrior brother feels left out," he said. "Why don't ye go show him how grateful ye are that he won the Games?"

I didn't understand at first, but Fergus angled his body so I saw Wulfgar, watching from the other side of the table with a slight grin.

Nodding, I got to my feet. The closer I got to the warrior, the larger he seemed. Yet his eyes were kind. Why had I been so afraid of him?

I lay my hand along the stubbled jaw, studying the rugged lines of his face. Had I once thought him ugly? There was something compelling about his lips, his eyes, even his scar. He wasn't good looking, not quite. But his looks were still pleasing.

"I'm going to kiss you," I whispered.

His eyes crinkled in an almost smile, but he didn't move. Even his arms stayed lax at his side as I bent and touched my lips to his. It was my first kiss where I was totally in control. I tilted my head and used my lips to coax his into softness. My nipples ruched tight and I longed to press my body against his great torso and relieve their tingling.

Instead I broke away to search his expression. "Did I do it right?"

His chuckle warmed me to my toes. "Exactly right. Now Fergus is going to give you your reward."

"Muriel, come sit in front of me."

The redheaded warrior waited for me on the bed. He scooted back as I came, making room for me to nestle on his lap facing Wulfgar. Once I was in position, Fergus drew my legs apart.

"Keep these where I put them, or you'll be punished."

My knees had already started to drift together. "Punished? How?"

"Fergus will bend you over the bed and spank your bare bottom," Wulfgar answered from his seat by the fire. He sipped from a horn, enjoying the show.

"What?" I craned my head to blink at the young man. "You would do that?"

"Oh yes. I'd enjoy it. Hearing ye gasp and beg, watching your bottom get all hot and red for me."

Again I didn't know if they were joking, so I just did as they said and let my legs fall back open.

"Wider," Wulfgar rasped from his chair. He leaned forward, elbows to knees, looking so intently at the place between my legs I wanted to squirm away.

"Here, sweet one, I'll help ye," Fergus hooked my legs over his knees, holding them wide.

I realized Wulfgar could see everything about me. Picking up a pelt, I held it against my bare chest.

"None of that," Fergus drew my meager covering away. "Ye will never hide yourself from us."

"But, no one has ever seen me like this."

"It's all right. We are your mates. No one's ever touched ye either, right, sweetheart?" Fergus' fingers skimmed over my bare chest, rested at my belly where they strummed lightly, like I was a lute and he was a master player.

"No," I breathed.

"And other than us, no one ever will," Wulfgar growled. He wasn't watching passively. His whole body was tense, leaning forward against an invisible leash holding him back. My heart stuttered in my chest as I watched the predator rise in his eyes. "I've killed for less."

"See, Muriel," Fergus soothed, "You're safe with us. We won't let anything happen to ye."

"But--"

"Hush now, and let me give ye pleasure." Fergus' fingers resumed their dance over my skin, everything in me came roaring to life.

"Do you remember what I taught you, Fergus?" Wulfgar's voice sounded strained.

"Aye. Now, Muriel, relax," Fergus breathed into my ear as his hand smoothed down the top of my thigh, and glided to the center. I tightened automatically, starting to close my legs before I remembered his order.

"Breathe, Muriel," Wulfgar commanded. "Nice and deep. In...and out." Focusing on his command distracted me for a moment.

With forked fingers, Fergus rubbed slowly up and down my nether lips. I whimpered.

"Wulfgar is going to watch while I pleasure ye. Would ye like that?" Fergus whispered.

"Yes."

"Do ye like making us happy? Do ye want to please your mates?" he continued stroking me, his voice a hypnotic murmur in my ear.

"Yes," I sighed, giving myself over to the sensation, a

tightness building within me, a wanting. My hips arched towards his touch.

"We are going to claim ye in every way, so ye know ye are ours."

"Please."

"Please what, wee one?"

"Please claim me. I want to be yours."

Teeth nipped my ear followed by a tongue to lave the hurt. His fingers never stopped moving.

A low sound filled the cabin, and I realized it was me. I was moaning. My legs tensed against his and he set them further apart.

"Beg me, sweetness. Beg for what ye want."

"I want..." My hips rocked on air. I didn't know what to want, beyond his perfect, continuous touch.

Wulfgar watched from a distance, his eyes gleaming. I wanted to rise up, beautiful and desired, and go to him. I would whirl and dance for his favor. I wanted to please my mates.

"What do ye want, Muriel? Should I stop?" Fergus' hand stilled and I grabbed it.

"No--"

"No? Ye don't make demands here, Muriel. We're in charge."

"Please don't stop. Do what you will." I thought frantically for what he'd want to hear. "I'm yours."

His chuckle gusted in my ear. "This is how ye will take your pleasure, always. At our hands. Desperate, pleading. Ye will beg, every time, and long for us to fill ye. And then, and only then, will we give ye your release."

"No," my voice grew faint. "Please. Please, I must—I need—" The pressure between my legs built, growing too large for my slender body to hold. Fergus' rasping voice and steady, continuous touch turned my body into a vessel filled with desire, ready to overflow.

"She grows close," Wulfgar growled.

A keening cry filled my ears, and after a second, I realized it came from me.

"Cum for me, Muriel. Cum now." At Fergus' command, I broke against his body, jerking like a leaf caught in a gale. His muscled arms steadied me even as his fingers plucked my nipples and fucked my cunny, driving my orgasm on and on.

When at last I grew still, sweat glistened on my bare flesh. Fergus fed me his wet fingers, and I did not protest licking them clean.

"Ye did not last very long. I had hoped to keep ye on edge for some time. We will have to work on that, wee one."

I collapsed back against his chest.

"Well done," Wulfgar told Fergus. "With time, you'll learn her signs so you can take her to the brink and keep her there, stimulating her higher and higher. The longer she waits, the more intense her climax will be."

"If I let her climax quickly, can I stimulate her again?"

"Yes, but very gently. Her tissues are sensitive to the touch."

Fergus brushed my folds once again, and my lower half spasmed.

"See? There are ways to keep pleasuring her but we have time to explore them. Today is merely the beginning." Wulfgar continued. "Place the heel of your hand on her and press lightly. Ground her. And always hold her afterwards. In these moments she is at peace, and most receptive to your touch."

"She's always receptive to my touch, aren't ye, sweetling?" Fergus trailed his fingers along the tops of my thighs. I shivered, but he only cupped the apex of my legs, holding me as Wulfgar had instructed. Completely held and cherished, I floated in my young lover's arms.

The door scraped as Wulfgar left the cabin, startling me awake. "Is it time now for me to pleasure you?"

"Soon, sweetness," Fergus shifted further back on the bed, lying down with me tucked in front of him. "But not when ye are so taken by the drink. We want your wits about ye when we claim ye, so ye can remember all ye learn."

I snuggled back against him, yawning even though I'd slept most the day. "If I do not learn quickly enough, will you punish me?"

"Perhaps," he laughed, and ground his cock into my bottom. "But those punishments ye will enjoy."

4

When I woke again it was to my warrior's murmuring. Their voices sounded strange, echoey and far away.

"Already he is moving among the pack, gaining support," Wulfgar said, and somehow I knew he was speaking of Siebold. "We must complete the mating bond; the sooner the better. I wish to be able to prove that we are bonded, in case he challenges me."

"Surely he won't challenge ye outright, not after ye beat him."

"Not for dominance. But he will make a case that he might be Muriel's true mate."

"Impossible," Fergus snorted. "That idiot couldn't bond with a horny goat, not even with a cock up his arse."

"You and I know it, but the pack..,"

"The pack knows it, too."

"The pack does not care if Siebold has a chance or not," Wulfgar continued patiently, "but once he puts the idea in their head, they will wonder if they might have a chance to try to mate with her. They will protest the Games. The Alphas may have no choice but to test our mate bond, and pass Muriel on if it does not hold."

"Never," Fergus said with a curse. "I will kill every last one of them to keep her, or die in the attempt."

"As would I. We must make sure it does not come to that."

"So we bond with her." I imagined Fergus shrugging. "She wants us. We want her. What's to stop us from mating?"

"She wants you. She still fears me. She has seen me as a monster."

"She'll come around."

"Never forget, Fergus, there's a beast inside us wanting to break free. We must never lose control, even when she comes to know that part of us, and accept it." Wulfgar paused. "She's awake."

"Muriel?" the door scraped open as he entered the hut. "Open your eyes, sweetheart. 'Tis time for another meal."

He made no mention of what they had been speaking of. My guts were twisting with fear of Siebold's schemes, but I kept my expression blank.

"Good morning," I stretched out on the bed, and the sight of my bare form in the pelts seemed to distract him from my eavesdropping.

He fell over me, holding himself up with hands on either side of my shoulders and slowly lowering himself atop me. His mouth came to mine and his kiss made me forget all the disturbing things I'd heard.

"'Tis not morning, but late afternoon."

"It feels like a new day," I smiled. "Besides, it can't be past noon. All I've done is eat and sleep."

"That is what these first few days are for," Wulfgar called. "To live together and learn one another."

"And fuck," Fergus added with a grin.

"We haven't done that."

"Not yet," but he pushed himself off and helped me up, leading me to the table still laden with food.

"Come sit with me, little one," Wulfgar pushed his chair back to make room. "It is my turn to feed you." With barely a hesitation, I obeyed. With my hands in my lap, I balanced on the giant warrior's knee, opening my mouth like a little bird for him to place food inside.

Fergus and Wulfgar chatted about the quality of the meat and mead, and did not speak of Siebold again.

As food hit my belly and the cobwebs cleared, what they'd spoken of sank in. We had to form a mating bond, and it seemed time was of the essence. I wished I had one of my sister's to consult with.

Learn one another, Wulfgar had said. That was my duty.

"How did you two meet?" I asked at the next pause in conversation.

"A long time ago," Fergus said, after he and Wulfgar exchanged amused glances.

"How old are you?"

"I was sixteen when I was Changed."

Wulfgar grunted dissent. "Fifteen if you were a day."

"I was skinny," Fergus argued. "My master never fed me." He addressed me again. "A band of Berserkers saw me being beaten. I was a slave."

"He stood up to his master, though. Defended a woman and took her place under his master's fists. I stepped in to stop it," Wulfgar said.

"Later that night my master came to do other things, worse things to me, and I fought back. He knifed me, threw me out, and left me for dead. Wulfgar came across my body and Changed me."

Noticing Wulfgar's cup was empty, I lifted the flagon, and at his nod, refilled it. "I thought the Change came by a witch's curse?"

"Sometimes, a man bitten by a one of us turns into a monster."

"You aren't monsters," I defended.

Pain flashed through Wulfgar's face. "No?"

I remembered Wulfgar's beast,the horror between man and wolf, standing over the mauled form of his enemies, and clutched the flagon to my chest.

Fergus balanced his chair on its back legs, enthralled with his own tale. "When I woke, I was Changed. I could run as a wolf. Wulfgar taught me to fight, and how to call the beast," Fergus smiled, and firelight glinted off his white, white teeth. "I made sure my old master never hurt anyone again. Left him lying in a pool of his own blood."

Wulfgar cleared his throat. "Perhaps Muriel need not hear the details of your first kill." Gently, the large warrior pried the flagon from my stone hands.

Fergus let the chair's front legs hit the floor with a bump. "Come sit with me, Muriel."

This was Fergus, I reminded myself. The friendly young warrior who flirted from the first time he saw me. He proffered his hand; I took it and let him pull me into his lap.

"Anyway, that is the story on how we came to meet."

"Is that when you formed a brother bond?"

"Not exactly."

"Do many warriors bond with one another?"

"A few. Our Alphas share a brother bond," Wulfgar went on, "as well as a bond with the whole pack, and now a mating bond with your sister Brenna. The mating bond is the most precious to us, because it is the only thing that allows us to control the beast completely. But, before we met you, the brother bond allowed us to help each other stave off madness. It strengthened over time."

"How did your bond form?"

"A brother bond forms when one wolf saves another," Fergus said.

"So you saved his life?" I twined my arms around his neck. His hands traveled up and down my body, and I cared not where they went.

"I did," Fergus said. "Many times, I recall."

"Truly?" Even though he was a strapping young man, Fergus seemed so slight compared to Wulfgar's hulking form.

"Yes," Fergus seemed annoyed at my surprise. "I lent my strength to him so he could win a challenge. How do ye think he won the Games?"

"So you lost on purpose?"

Fergus' cheeks turned pink, clashing with his hair. Wulfgar laughed outright.

"The agreement was that I would fall out of the Games early, and hide in the woods, giving aid through the bond we share."

"Amazing. Do all bonds work the same?"

"We do not know. We don't speak of these private bonds much with the pack."

I took a deep breath and asked the question that had been weighing on me. "So how do we form a mating bond?"

Fergus glanced at Wulfgar, who confirmed with a nod.

"Wee one, we will show ye...now."

I couldn't help but feel nervous as Fergus lifted me from his lap. He carried me to the bed and set me down to strip off his leather jerkin. The sight of his bare chest, sprinkled with coarse hair, distracted me from my apprehension.

"Do ye remember how I touched ye?"

"Yes."

"Touch yerself, now. Do it slow, as we like."

I nodded and parted my legs.

"This touch will quicken ye and make ye slick with your honey. It will ease my cock."

As I stroked my folds, Fergus tugged off his breeches and knelt on the bed. His hair hung down to his shoulders, brushing the freckled muscles. If I focused on him, I could pretend we were alone, two young lovers exploring each other.

"Kiss me, sweetheart," he breathed, and I closed my eyes, winding my free hand around him. In the end I lay on my back with Fergus between my splayed legs.

"You're beautiful, just as I imagined."

I blushed.

His hands ran over my body to tug my nipples. Cream gushed over my hand at the slight pain.

"Ye like that? Ye enjoy when I pinch ye?"

I would've denied it, but he did it again and my hips jerked in wanton invitation.

His expression turned triumphant. "These are mine now," he squeezed a handful of each breast. "I may never allow ye to wear clothes again."

"Fergus—" my protest broke off when he bent and set his mouth over one pink tipped mound, sucking the nipple into his mouth. When he lifted his head my nipple remained peaked and red as a berry.

I pushed at his shoulder but was helpless to stop him as he subjected the other nipple to the same treatment.

"Fighting me already?" he murmured against my skin.

"No, Fergus, I just—"

His teeth scraped my breast and sensation shot through me, straight to my soaked cunny.

"Ye like that..."

"No—"

"Dinnae deny it." His fingers found my cleft and pushed mine aside. "You're wet for me."

"Fergus, please—" Pleasure coiled down below, tension tightening between my hips with each stroke of my fingers.

"Stop." He caught my wrist and I whimpered as the building sensation dissipated, leaving a fierce ache.

"Hands above your head, Muriel," he ordered. "Don't make me tell ye twice."

Eyes wide, I obeyed. My lover seemed to transform, growing larger and broader, his handsome jaw set in a determined expression.

"Fergus," Wulfar called in a warning tone.

"It's all right, Muriel," He spoke to me but seemed to be reassuring his warrior brother. "I will never hurt ye."

"I know," I whispered.

"Keep your hands there, or I'll tie them down. I want to...explore."

Hot breath blew over my skin and it was all I could do to keep my hands where they were. Fergus took his time kissing my breasts, soothing away the lingering pain. I wanted more than anything to touch him, but when I moved my hand, he growled, pinning me.

Wulfgar loomed over the bed. "Careful," he told his fellow warrior. "Be sure to keep control."

"I will."

I caught the pained expression on Wulfgar's face before Fergus' hands tightened on my wrists, drawing my attention back to him. His hips dipped and the ridge of his cock brushed my lower lips. I arched up to press against the hard length.

"That's it, rock against me," Fergus ordered.

I closed my eyes as I obeyed, but still saw Wulfgar's strained expression in my mind's eye. Why wasn't he taking part? Had my nervous inexperience made him uncomfortable?

My movements stilled. Fergus released one of my wrists and slid a hand between us to check my slit. "You're wet, but not wet enough."

"Let me see to her." Wulfgar said. A shadow fell over me as he came closer. I did my best not to flinch away.

Fergus moved, seating himself behind me and cradling me in his lap.

"What are we doing?" I asked, just as Wulfgar knelt down and propped my legs on his shoulders.

I squirmed and Fergus' arms closed around me, holding me still and shackling my wrists with gentle hands.

"Be still, sweet one. Ye don't need to know what's happening. Ye just need to obey."

Wulfgar bent forward and hot breath gusted over my secret parts. My lower half jerked.

The large warrior between my legs started kissing up the tender skin of my inner thighs.

Fergus restrained me when I would surge up off the bed. Between his arms around me and Wulfgar's hold on my legs, I was well and truly helpless.

"She likes being held down," Wulfgar said, gaze fixed on my swollen folds. "Even as she squirms, her cunny pours forth cream." Dipping his head, he lapped it up.

"Oh please." My head fell back. I couldn't move, couldn't do more than beg—and feel. Wulfgar's tongue lapped up and down my plump lower lips, as if he couldn't get enough.

The softness of his mouth and rasp of his stubble had me twitching with pleasure.

Fergus reaffirmed his grip, making sure I couldn't move. Somehow knowing I couldn't escape made the sensations between my legs more powerful. I could only be still, and feel.

Wulfgar's tongue flicked a sensitive spot over and over, until I was moaning.

Fergus shushed me, palming my breast. "You're not to cum until I say. Otherwise ye will be punished."

"Punished? How?" I managed to gasp out. Wulfgar paused, allowing me to get my thoughts in order. "You speak often of punishing me. I wish to know more." Fergus seemed to look forward to punishing me. His excitement made me curious.

"Dinnae tempt me, sweet one. Ye will know, soon enough."

Wulfgar returned to his work, sweeping his tongue up my slit and I lost all sense. My hips bucked and writhed but Wulfgar held them fast and my struggles did nothing to budge his large hands. Little shocks ran through me, from the mouth on my cunt to the fingers on my nipples.

Fergus kept up his savage litany, "Ye willnae cum, ye must hold back. Naughty lassies who take their pleasure without permission get punished."

His words made me ache with pleasure, even as I fought to obey. I was a good girl. I had to hold back. My muscles clenched, but that only made me slide closer to the edge. Wulfgar slipped a finger into my fluttering hole, and then another. The slight stretch burned and yet I clamped down on his fingers, longing for more.

"Please," I gasped.

"That's it. Beg him. Say his name," Fergus encouraged.

I directed my pleas to the shaved head at my center. "Wulfgar, please. I can't....I need..." Pressure mounted in my mind, and I lost the ability to speak.

Just as I was at the tipping point, almost buried under an avalanche of pleasure, Wulfgar raised his head. To my embarrassment, his face was slick with my juices.

"She's ready. It's time."

Fergus scooted out from under me, and I found myself lying under him, looking up into his eager face.

"I'm gonna fuck ye now," he said, eyes bright gold. "I'll go slowly, so I don't hurt ye."

I was already reaching for him, longing for the press of his hard body against mine. His hands slid down my sides, spanning my small waist as he drank in the sight of me.

"So lovely. I've waited for this a long, long time."

"Please, Fergus." I wound my arms around him and he lowered himself. He came into me, the tip of his cock pressing forward with that slow, burning sensation. It hurt and satisfied at the same time. Because Wulfgar had prepared me, I expected the slight discomfort. I wrapped my legs around him and tried to tug him forward.

"No, lovely. We go slowly. It may hurt."

"Please, Fergus, just thrust inside."

"Nay, wee one," he chastened, but pushed forward another half inch anyway. I caught my breath. He paused and let me stretch around him.

"So large," I grunted, and caught his delighted expression. He slid out and back in, each time going a bit further. I found myself raising my hips and digging my nails into his back, hanging on for dear life even as I asked for more.

His cock slid forward and I clenched around him—to keep him in or to shut him out, I did not know.

With a gasp he slammed forward. A twinge of pain made

me go still, but he was moving now, rocking in and out, his cock sliding easily on my juices.

"Sorry, lass. I couldnae help it. I need ye."

I crooned reassurances and tightened my legs around his back, drawing him closer. We stared into each other's eyes as he thrust, his movements growing easier.

"Oh, lass, I love the feel of ye."

In answer I twined my arms tighter around his shoulders. He kissed and sucked on the spot where my shoulder met my neck. Teeth grazed my tender skin just as Fergus swiveled his hips, rubbing against the sensitive place that Wulfgar had licked to life. Pleasure shot through me.

"Oh," I cried. My muscles clenched and it was too much for Fergus. He bucked between my legs, calling my name. Cheeks flushed, he pulled out with a shudder.

"She's not done," Wulfgar hovered over the bed, and I remembered he was there, watching us. "Use your thumb. Flick at the nub, there. Light, and fast."

"Look at me, Muriel," Fergus ordered. I held his gaze and the intense light combined with the fluttering touch sent me over the edge. I gasped and flopped like a woman possessed. The men's satisfied expression told me they were pleased with me.

Fergus pulled out and I saw a little watery blood on the pelts. Wulfgar came and laid a warm cloth over my center. I blushed, knowing how he'd tasted me intimately.

"Sore?" he asked.

I nodded, still shy around this great warrior. He helped me sit up and sip from a horn of water. He was so large, I felt like a mere girl in his arms. His hard length pressed into my bottom, and I wondered what it would feel like to take him inside me. I'd thought Fergus was too large, but my body had stretched around him and in the end, we fitted like we were made for each other. Would it be the same with Wulfgar? A part of me was eager to find out, even as I quailed at the thought. When I rose from his lap, I paused in the circle of his arms. He simply held me, making no move to press himself onto my body. Yet I could tell his cock was ready. He'd watched the whole time, and not taken his release. Had I done something wrong?

In a small voice, I asked, "What about you? Are you going to...take your pleasure?"

Wulfgar shook his head. "Not this time, sweet one." Bending his head, he caught my chin between two rough fingers and gave me a thorough kiss.

But that was all he took. When Fergus came to pull me into his arms, Wulfgar rose and left the cabin. I frowned but relaxed into my young lover's hold.

"So is that it? Are we bonded now?"

"Why do ye ask? Are ye going to run to the Alphas and ask for a new mate?"

"No, of course not, I just—"

He squeezed me close. "I was only teasing ye. You're stuck with us, whether we bond in a day or in a week."

"But it needs to be soon, right?"

Rolling, Fergus positioned us both on our sides, facing each other. He studied my face.

"Where did you hear that?"

I didn't want to admit to eavesdropping, so I shrugged. "From my sisters."

"The sooner the better, but it's not for ye to worry about. Trust your mates to handle it. Ye just focus on pleasing us."

I gnawed my lip a moment, and then gave in. "All right. How do I do that?"

A grin spread over his face. "Kiss me, for a start."

We lay in bed, drinking in one another's presence.

Fergus wooed me softly with long, drugging kisses until I melted into the bed.

A sharp sound outside had me tense. "What's that?"

"'Tis only Wulfgar, chopping wood."

"Is he all right?"

"Of course," Fergus brushed aside my concerns.

"I had hoped to please him," I bit my lip.

"Ye will. Ye do," Fergus said, but he rose, grabbing up his breeches and dressing. "We can go to him, if ye wish."

"I can't. I have no dress," I pointed out, and Fergus lifted his leather jerkin.

"Ye may wear something of mine."

"But...that will barely cover me."

"Exactly."

Rolling my eyes, I slid out of bed and dressed as he wished. The tunic was large on me but barely came to my thighs. There was nothing to stop my new mate from sliding his hand under the leather and gripping my bottom; which is exactly what he did.

I protested, but my nipples hardened, rubbed to points under the heavy fabric.

"Fergus?"

"Yes, my love?"

"When exactly did your bond with Wulfgar form?"

"I helped him kill a warrior."

My eyes widened. "One of the pack?"

"Yes. The Berserker madness took him. The beast claimed his mind and he never recovered."

"Does that happen often?"

"Not since ye and your sisters came," he planted a light kiss on my temple. "Which is why ye are so precious, Muriel. Ye tame the beast. Let it sleep. We're part wolf, part man, and part pure, raging desire. We call that part the beast."

"What does the beast desire?"

"Surrender." He pulled me closer, kneading my bottom. The jerkin rode up to my hips as he put his between mine. I didn't care, I shamelessly ground myself down on his thigh. His teeth nipped at my ear. "And ye will give us what we want, every time."

He drew away suddenly and laughed at my bereft look. Even though I was sore between my legs, my body was hot and aroused, ready for more.

"That is why it's so important ye obey," he said in a more serious tone.

"Of course I obey," I huffed. "It's not like I can fight you."

A wicked light gleamed in his eyes. "Ye could try."

Squeezing my hand, Fergus dragged me out of the hut, past Wulfgar. The giant had stripped to his breeches and was using an axe to split wood for us. He turned to watch us go by.

"I'm teaching Muriel to fight," Fergus called. He brought me to a small clearing and handed me a large branch.

"What am I going to do with this?"

"Hit me." Fergus practically bounced on his feet. His excitement was contagious.

Dutifully, I gripped the branch and tried to swipe at him. Fergus caught my clumsy blow and backed up a pace. "That's it. Come at me again, but place your hands further apart on your staff."

After a few minutes, I was sweating, but my blows were tighter and less unwieldy.

"Does this help our bond?" I asked.

Fergus rolled his eyes. "'Tis fun. Ye worry to much about the bond."

I bit my tongue before I revealed what I knew and snapped that my worry was for him. That Siebold would take his life. Instead, I drove myself forward with bolder thrusts and parries. Fergus blocked them with his arms, a wide grin on his face.

Wulfgar left his axe to come and watch. "Good work, Muriel. Keep it up and you'll be better than he is."

I started to thank him, and Fergus darted in, plucking the branch right out of my hands.

"Hey!"

"Ye put your back to me. First rule. Always remain alert."

Fergus dropped the branch and danced away. I lunged for my makeshift weapon. Lifting it, I began to advance, altering my steps so I drove Fergus back, straight to where Wulfgar was waiting.

At the last moment, Fergus realized what I was doing and ducked, but not before Wulfgar side swiped him with a giant paw. The duck and feint quickly turned into a brawl between the larger warrior and the younger.

I dropped the branch and backed away. Feet turned to monster's claws and dug into the ground. Their upper torsos remained human, arms wrapped around each other in a wrestler's stance.

For such a smaller warrior, Fergus held his own ground. He moved quickly, slipping out of Wulfgar's hold and dancing around him.

With a roar, Wulfgar lunged, grabbing the smaller wolf around his middle and flinging him to the ground. Fergus hit the grass and rolled, coming up with teeth snapping. His fingers stiffened, his hands growing into large paws tipped with curved claws.

I gave a frightened squeak.

Suddenly, two warriors were looking at me with blazing,

feral eyes. I backed away slowly, raising my stick in paltry defense. They strode forward, Fergus knocking my weapon from my hands and Wulfgar scooping me right up, so I hung over his shoulder.

"Our prize," he growled, and headed back to our hovel.

Inside he set me down. I waited, wringing my hands as they stripped out of their breeches.

Fergus came to me first.

"What—"

His hands, back to looking human, gripped the neck of the jerkin I wore and tore it down the front. I went still, but he just laughed. Stripping the remains of the leather shirt away, he tossed me onto the bed where I scrambled back, breathing hard.

"Calm yourself," Wulfgar rumbled. "We won't hurt ye. But we will take what's ours."

Fergus came to me and I made myself not flinch away. His fingers touched the center of my legs. "She's already wet and ready."

Anger surged through me. I had been frightened, and they were enjoying it. "Wait a minute." I set a hand against his chest.

"Ye going to fight now, wee one?" Fergus snapped his teeth. I pushed at him, and found myself flat on my back, faced with a wild creature. I stared into golden eyes and the beast stared back.

"Calm yourself, Fergus. Keep control."

Fergus whined, an animal sound, but he lifted off me. Wulfgar took his place, his eyes were just as bright. His muscles bulged as he held himself over me. Caged thus, I had no desire to fight.

"Please," I whispered, "I'll be good."

Nuzzling at my neck, Wulfgar found a sensitive spot. He sucked hard and I was undone.

Slowly, the warrior made his way down my body. His tongue sought my secret places, I gasped and writhed, but he would not let me up. Instead, he took my wrists and firmly pinned them.

The movement snapped something inside me, and pleasure flooded through me. I panted through my climax.

"Oh, Muriel, you're perfect," Fergus groaned. He had his cock sheathed in his hand and was slowly pulling on it.

"Be calm, little one. We will not hurt you." Wulfgar's teeth caught the sensitive spot where my neck and shoulder met and nipped, turning my body liquid. When he raised his head, his canines looked sharper. Much sharper.

But when he slid his fingers down to check my folds, I whimpered. I was still sore.

"You're not ready yet." Wulfgar backed away. His cock jutted from his body, red and angry.

"I'm sorry," I whispered. I wanted to roll over and bury my face in the pelts.

"It's not your fault, little one." Wulfgar grabbed a pelt and dropped it to the floor. "Would you still like to please us?"

I nodded and he pointed to a place at his feet. "Come kneel here."

Once I did, I looked up at his stiff member. The broad head held a drop of liquid at its tip.

Gathering my hair, Wulfgar drew me closer.

"Lick it," he ordered. "Lots of tongue. Get it nice and wet."

I did so, hesitant at first. The flavor was salty but not unpleasant. I ran my tongue up and down his cock, and lapped at the tip until his breath hissed out.

"Grip it in your hand. Gentle." My hand looked small and delicate against the slick rod. He showed me how to work up and down his length. On a whim I leaned forward and put my mouth over the tip.

"Oh Muriel" It was his turn to groan. I almost smiled at my new-found power. No longer hesitating, I swirled my tongue over the broad head while my hand slid up and down.

Wulfgar's larger hand closed over mine and he jerked in a faster rhythm that I continued when he took his hand away.

His large sack grew tighter and with my other hand I touched it, fascinated. "Oh, yes. Touch me again. Like that."

I cupped and fondled him, stopping to wet his cock with my mouth from time to time. He kept his hand in my hair but did not tug or hurt me. His movements were careful, gentle, as if I was as fragile as a flower.

"Do I please you, sir?" I asked in an innocent tone.

Behind us, Fergus cursed loudly, and I knew he'd cum.

"Oh, yes, little one. You please me." Wulfgar's eyes glowed.

Closing my mouth over his cock, I sucked hard. My hand sped its movements. I knew he was close when his head fell back and he sighed, no longer able to give orders or do anything but enjoy my ministrations.

"One day we'll teach ye to take us fully in your mouth," Fergus said. "We'll sheath our cocks in your throat and you'll swallow us down. Do ye like the sound of that?"

My bare cunny was swollen and dripping on the floor. The thought of serving my men set my body tingling.

"Mmhmm," I hummed over Wulfgar's cock, answering without removing my mouth. The great warrior cursed.

"You'll wake us each morning with your mouth," Fergus

continued in a heated whisper. "And once we've cum, we'll give ye pleasure over and over, then leave ye in bed, covered in our seed."

I moaned at the wanton image. The words filled me with blazing desire, and I wanted nothing more than to be covered in my men's seed.

"Ah, Muriel," Wulfgar panted. "I'm cumming...soon..."

"Suck him, Muriel, suck him hard." Fergus bent close to me. "Do your best to please him or you'll be punished." His fingers pinched my nipples and the pain made me gasp. The excited sound pushed Wulfgar over the edge.

He spurted over and over onto my bare chest. Reaching down, he rubbed his seed into my skin, leaving a pearly cast.

"Good girl," he told me. Then I was up, up, lifted and spread out on the bed, and the two men saw to my swollen cunny over and over again.

"WHY DOES WULFGAR NOT FUCK ME?" I asked Fergus that night. The giant warrior had gone to patrol the woods, leaving us until dawn. For fun, Fergus made a nest of pelts near the hearth, close enough for him to easily roll a log into the fire. We cuddled and kissed for a time, and now I rested on his firm chest, playing with the ruddy hairs and tracing his freckles.

"He is being careful. He has spent a long time learning to control his beast. He doesnae want to hurt ye."

I frowned. "But how will we bond?"

To my surprise, Fergus leaned down and smacked my bare bottom, lightly, but hard enough to make a smacking sound. "Enough, lass," he said with mock gruffness. "You're too worried about the bond. Pester me about it again, and there'll be consequences."

I rolled my eyes.

The next thing I knew, Fergus had me up and over his lap.

"Fergus! What are you doing?" I squirmed but he pinned me easily, shifting me so my bum draped right over his legs. He smacked it again and I squawked, though it didn't hurt at all.

"Punishing ye," he said, and I could hear the grin in his tone. "This is how wolves discipline their naughty mates." His hand roamed over my naked flesh, squeezing my plump cheeks.

"It doesn't hurt very much--Ow!"

His palm connected with my right buttcheek, hard enough to sting. I reared up but didn't go far, as Fergus pushed me down with a strong hand. "And another to balance ye out." Another smack rang out and I jerked my hands back to cover my now stinging backside.

My love caught my wrists and held them in the small of my back.

"Enough, Fergus, I've learned my lesson."

"Ah, but now I am enjoying myself." His free hand went back to massaging my bottom, reducing the sting. He continued like that, alternating his caresses with a light spanking. I whimpered once or twice, but submitted to his ministrations. As the playful punishment went on, my cunny began to pulse with each firm smack. Burying my face in the pelts, I let my legs creep together so Fergus would not see the wetness at their apex.

Of course, Fergus noticed right away.

"What's this, lass? I think you're enjoying your discipline as much as me."

"I am not," I protested, but his fingers slipped through my secret folds and then showed me the juice collected on them.

"Lying lassies get their bottoms smacked."

I hung my head. "I only like it because it's you." To emphasize this, I wriggled, my stomach giving his cock its own massage.

Fergus chuckled, catching onto my game.

"So if I called Wulfgar back inside to punish ye, it willnae have the same effect?"

I stilled, imagining those giant hands clapping down on my frail buttocks.

"Calm yourself, Muriel. 'Twas merely joking." Fergus helped me up, his face serious. "Ye really are afraid of him."

"I'm not... not really." I dissembled, but I couldn't lie to a wolf like I could lie to myself. "He's just so big. And grand, and important in the pack."

"He is but a man. Am I not so big and grand to ye?"

I gulped, but Fergus was teasing. "You're my age, and I always wanted you."

"And I wanted ye. 'Tis fate, that we would become lovers and mated for all time." He swept the hair off my shoulder and gave me a kiss. I leaned into him, pushing closer to find his mouth and straddle him. The hardened lines of his muscled torso looked delicious enough to lick. I started to dip my head, my lips ready to explore, when he drew me back up.

"Promise me ye will give Wulfgar a chance."

"I am," I huffed. My cunny throbbed impatiently. "It's him who stays away from our bed at night. And neither of you will fuck me."

"We're waiting until you're healed." He pulled me down

onto the pelts and swung over me so his face was between my legs and his cock bobbed inches from my mouth.

"What are you doing?"

"Giving ye pleasure. First one to cum serves the other all night."

"But--" My words died as he lowered his head and covered my mons with his mouth. Hot and ready, I climaxed in mere seconds, and spent the rest of our time in front of the fire with Fergus' cock in my mouth or cradled between my breasts.

5

A week passed with us living in isolation. During the day we ate, played in the woods, practicing sparring. Most of the fighting or exploring turned into a game of the warriors hunting me down to have their way with me. Each time, they used their mouths to see to my tender folds, but did not fuck me again. Instead, I learned to suck them down to the hilt, just as Fergus told me. The easiest way was lying on the bed, head outstretched to take them all the way down in my throat, while they pinched my nipples.

I enjoyed myself so much, I nearly forgot about the bond.

I woke one night in a tangle of pelts. My men were murmuring to each other again. I lay very still listening to their echoing voices. Their voices seemed far away, even though they sat not a few feet from me at the table in front of the fire.

"Five days, and she's still sore. I expected to have fucked my bride at least twenty times by now. Not that I don't enjoy her wee mouth."

"Calm yourself, Fergus. She was a virgin and unused to a man's touch."

"The magic should've helped her heal by now. It would've, if we were bonded. Would marking her speed the process?"

"Until we know she's bonded with us, we dare not mark her. The beast wants to bite her, claim her as ours, but teeth could hurt her unless she shares our ability to heal."

Fergus blew out a frustrated breath. The sound was louder and more clear than their conversation, but I did not have time to wonder at that.

"I would ask the Alphas for advice," mused Wulfgar, "but—"

"We dare not, brother. No one in the pack can know."

"Agreed. We'll think of something."

A chair creaked, and Wulfgar said, "I'll stand watch. Keep her warm, little brother."

"Are ye sure? Ye can take a turn with her." I heard the concern in his voice, and felt it in my own breast. Wulfgar had never spent the night in our bed.

"I'm sure," The door closed, but Wulfgar's voice didn't grow any fainter than it already was. "Take care of our little mate."

A few seconds later, Fergus sank onto the pelts next to me. His arms wrapped around me and he pulled me against his warm weight, and I rolled into him with a sigh.

His touch soothed some of what I'd heard but not much. A week had passed and we still had not bonded. Fergus said not to worry, but I had to do something. They could not hide me away forever, and keep their failed claiming a secret. Eventually the pack would find out. We needed to bond.

Fergus let out a gust of breath. He was already asleep, while I lay awake with thoughts twisting my mind. Both

Wulfgar and Fergus already shared a bond. The fault did not lie with them. It lay with me.

I had to fix this. If only I had asked Sabine more questions when I had the chance. I could ask to speak with Brenna now, but then she and the Alphas would know something was wrong.

As the minutes stretched to hours, I lay in the dark, gnawing my lip. There was one person I knew who was neither my sister or pack.

By morning, I decided.

I would find and speak to the witch.

MY CHANCE CAME when Wulfgar went to meet with the Alphas and left Fergus watching over me.

"Be good, little one."

"Always, sir," I told him, and offered my lips for a kiss. I still hadn't gotten over my shyness around the great warrior.

Fergus was another matter. The red-haired warrior pounced on me as soon Wulfgar disappeared into the trees. "What shall we do today?"

"I-I don't know." My mind raced as to how I could occupy my love while I did the ritual to summon the witch.

"I can think of a few things," Fergus had already tugged my gown off my shoulder, and was kissing my neck.

"Perhaps we can go to the river. I need to wash our clothes." Wulfgar had brought me two more gowns to replace my stained one, but one was already dirty and ripped from a time when Fergus had chased me through the forest and caught and used me for his pleasure.

"My cock needs washing," Fergus murmured. He took my earlobe between his teeth and nibbled. My body responded with a gush of liquid between my weakening legs.

"Fergus," I gave a nervous laugh. "Please."

"All right," he set me away. "But I will have ye see to me when you're done."

"Of course," I nodded eagerly, and he chuckled.

"Such a good girl."

"I try to be."

"Ye are. Ye please us so much." He caught my chin, studying my face as he often did before pronouncing me beautiful. I bit my lip. I longed to be a good mate for them. I had to be. This had to work.

To my relief, Fergus let me go to the river. He even carried the basket of dirty clothes, but once there, instructed me to stay on the bank, changed into his wolf, and started distracting himself by fishing, wolf-style.

He waited over a deep pool, intent on the water until the right moment. With a leap, he'd rear up and, with legs stiff before him, snap his head down into the water. If he was lucky, he'd have a slim fish in his jaws. He came up empty more often than not, but the activity amused him. Quietly laying out the ingredients for the ritual, I was grateful that he was distracted.

After awhile he grew bored and lay down to nap in the sun, and I crept away, around the riverbend, a little out of sight of the sleeping wolf. I hated sneaking around, but Sabine had told me that even though the Alphas consulted with her often, most Berserkers didn't like the witch. I couldn't risk telling Fergus and Wulfgar, and have them forbid me to summon her. Besides, I didn't want them to know how worried I was about the mating bond.

At the foot of a tree, I built a little fire and did the summoning spell Sabine had taught me.

"Yseult," I called the witch's name, and waited.

Minutes passed and I stayed still, resisting the urge to creep back to check on Fergus, or repeat the spell.

At last, I gave up waiting and blew the fire out. The witch was not coming. I had failed. Perhaps I had no magical abilities, and this was why I could not form a mating bond with Wulfgar and Fergus. My sister's powers made them perfect matches for the Berserkers, but I had none. Good, sweet Muriel who always did as she was told. I'd finally been given everything my heart desired, but I wasn't good enough to keep it.

The one decision that remained: did I tell Fergus and Wulfgar of my failing, or spend as long as I could living my dream, and let them find out for themselves, and cast me aside?

Tears pricked my eyes as I packed up the remnants of the spell, and kicked the fire to death.

I startled as a raven landed on a branch above my head and cawed. It flapped its wings and glided to my feet. I leapt back, and it landed, and cocked a beady eye at me.

"Yseult?" I asked.

The raven cawed again, and instead of feeling foolish, hope leaped up in me.

Then the bird flew away.

"No, wait," I ran after it, crashing into the forest undergrowth, pushing aside branches to see where it might have gone. No sooner than I started after it, I lost it, and was left standing in the forest, wondering if I'd failed again.

"Foolish girl," I told myself, and started to go back, when a low growl caught my ear. Peering into the sun-dappled darkness, I saw the wolf.

The animal was large, white with golden streaks. Feet rooted to the spot, I thought fast. Wulfgar's wolf was grey,

Fergus was red. This beast was a stranger to me. It tilted its head, and the light caught its golden eyes. A Berserker.

When I backed away, the wolf paced forward, pushing through the thick brush with nary a sound. I turned and ran. Racing, weaving through trees, I dared not look back to see if the hunter was on my trail.

"Fergus," I screamed. "Fergus." The stream bank came into sight, and he bounded forward, in man form.

"Muriel..." he caught me.

"Wolf. In the forest."

"I see," he growled, placing himself between the forest and me. "If any creature attacks, ye run as fast a ye can, back to the hut."

My fingers dug into his sides. If something attacked, I could not be sure I could leave him.

"What did I say to ye about leaving my sight?"

"I'm s-sorry," I stuttered.

"Never mind," he grabbed my hand and pulled me along. We left the laundry along the bank and raced back to the hut.

"I'm sorry," I said again, once I'd caught my breath. "I know I saw a wolf. It started to track me, so I ran."

"I have no doubt ye saw something. There are probably spies in this wood."

"Spies?"

"Never mind." Fergus turned to me from barring the door. "What were ye doing?"

"I needed an herb and thought I might find it on the edge of the forest." It wasn't a lie, not quite. It wasn't just the whole truth. Fergus' head tilted as he regarded my words. I wondered if he knew I was hiding something.

"When we lived in the village, I foraged unguarded," I supplied. "I did not think there would be a danger."

"You're an intelligent lass. Does it make sense that ye go off alone?"

My gaze fell to my feet. "No."

"Muriel. Look at me." There was no tender seduction in my young lover. "Ye live among the Berserkers now, and we expected ye to act seemly as our mate. I told ye to stay close. When Wulfgar returns, he will lecture ye on the same thing."

I needed no more cause to dread the intimidating warrior. "Do you have to tell him?"

"I hide nothing from him. And neither should ye, as his mate."

My heart sank. I'd meant to bring the three of us closer together, and instead I'd made a mess of things. "I'm sorry."

With a sigh, Fergus opened his arms. "Come here." When I was safe in his hold, he continued, "I forgive ye, but ye must make amends." Gathering a fistful of hair, he gently drew my head back. "I'm going to punish ye now."

There was no joking in his manner. I swallowed hard. "A-all right."

My head was pounding as Fergus lead me to the bed. "Dress off."

I'd gotten used to hearing this order; Fergus preferred me naked whenever we were in the cabin. As I pulled the gown over my head, he sat and patted his knee.

"Lie over my lap."

I hesitated.

"'Tis better to complete your punishment before Wulfgar returns. He might wish to strap ye."

That was enough to send me scuttling into place. Fergus helped me drape across his legs, steadying me as I settled into position.

"Good lass," he said quietly. "This spanking isnae for fun, but punishment."

I sniffed, my lower lip trembling as I squeezed the bedclothes and tried not to cry. I was upset, not because I was afraid of the spanking, but because I'd disappointed him.

The first swat focused my thoughts. Fergus spanked me hard, nothing like the soft swats he'd used in my last, playful punishment.

"This punishment will remind ye to heed my words." Fergus' lecture accompanied his slaps. I winced and gritted my teeth against the sting. "Ye will not stray from our sight again. To do so is verrae, verrae dangerous. Wulfgar won the Games, but his claim to ye is still contested."

I raised my head at that, but he finished with a flurry of smacks that had me gasping and kicking my feet. "It's very important that ye not sneak off. Promise me that ye willnae do so again."

"I promise."

"Ten more." The final swats seemed harder than all the rest combined. The cabin resonated with the smacking sound. Gritting my teeth, I hung my head and let a tear or two fall. When it was over, I lay limp, waiting for him to help me up.

"Such a good, good girl." He kissed and cuddled me, angling me onto my side so my weight didn't rest on my sore bottom. Even with my body singing with pain, I wanted to snuggle close to my young warrior. The tightness in my chest was gone.

"Punishment's over. Ye are forgiven." Fergus wiped the last tear from my eye. His thumb dropped to my lips and stroked them until I opened my mouth and sucked it inside.

"Good lass," his voice turned gravelly, and I squirmed in

his lap for a different reason. When I went to stand, he grunted and pulled me, winding his strong arms around me. I pushed at him to no avail. His eyes glowed with an unearthly light, and I knew his beast was enjoying my struggle.

"You like punishing me."

"I do. But only because it pleases me to have ye submit to it so prettily."

"Does it please the wolf?"

"Aye, the wolf enjoys dominating ye, but 'tis the beast that enjoys your pain." He pinched my sore bottom and I hissed. "And your pleasure. It wants ye to forget where one ends and one begins." He tweaked my nether lips and a bolt of sensation shot through me. "We will give ye ecstasy beyond what ye have ever known, but ye will cry out and beg us to stop many, many times."

"And will you?" I held my breath as his fingers started to slide in and out of my slick opening, awakening every part of me to pleasure.

"Never. We are your masters, and we know what ye need."

He finger fucked me until I was begging him, then stopped and had me lick his fingers clean.

"I'll stop and bid ye raise your skirts from time to time. Make sure you're wet and ready for us. Keep ye on edge, begging."

He nodded to my hardened nipples.

"Pinch them."

I did and more cream seeped out from me. Lightning bolts of sensation shot from my nipples to my cunny, and I found my hips rocking where I sat. "Please."

"No," he laughed. "'Tis better to keep ye on edge, and wanting. Feel how hard I am."

He laid my palm over his throbbing length. "I love tormenting ye, and knowing ye suffer by my hand."

"Take me, Fergus," I begged. The fading sting in my bottom was nothing to the throbbing in my lady parts. "Make me feel that I am yours."

"Ye are mine. Ye belong to me forever." Just when I thought he'd throw me to the bed and fuck me, he set me on my feet and stood. "Come. Your punishment is not over."

He had me stand in the corner of the room, "To think on how ye will obey next time."

I shifted from foot to foot, and listened to him work in the room.

Minutes seemed like hours, but I did not turn around until he bade me.

"Wulfgar is soon to return, my lovely. It's time to begin your training."

"Training?" Still naked, I wrapped my arms loosely around my bare form. The look Fergus shot me was wicked.

"Bend over the bed."

I hurried to obey.

"Such a fine arse. Not too small, not too plump. And a lovely red color. Spread your legs, sweet one." I rocked from one foot to the other, opening my stance. "Good lass. Now part your bottom cheeks for me."

"Fergus—"

A smack on my behind had me hastening to comply. Flushing red as my punished backside, I spread my cheeks and showed him my bottom hole.

"Now there's a lovely sight," Fergus said with satisfied awe.

My face burned hot against the bed. Something hard and unyielding touched my back pucker, pushing in so it stretched the tight ring of muscle.

"This is a plug. I carved it out of wood for naughty lassies to wear when they've disobeyed. You'll keep it in, and it will stretch ye to take us."

My grip tightened on the pelts. "Fergus...please...:"

"Relax. Take a deep breath in. Now blow out." As air left my lungs, he pushed the bulb in all the way. After the widest part went through, it narrowed sharply, easing the strain.

"There."

He worked it in and out while I stifled a whimper.

"How do ye feel?"

I grunted in response. The thing in my backside felt strange but not quite unpleasant. My nipples were as hard as pebbles against the bed.

"Touch yourself."

"Please...do not make me."

"If ye cannot, then I will." He checked me and laughed. "Soaked. Just as I thought."

"This is not right."

He dropped a kiss on my bottom cheek. "It is exactly right. Soon ye'll be able to wear this in your bottom from morn to night."

"All day?"

"Of course. So we can claim ye whenever we want."

He twisted the dreadful thing home. "Stand up now, Muriel. Ye can suck me off before ye continue with your chores."

I grimaced, knowing I would be denied pleasure until that night.

"Keep it in as long as I say, and ye will be rewarded."

"Yes, Fergus." I reached up and couldn't quite hide my eagerness as I guided his cock into my mouth.

∾

PLUG FIRMLY SEATED between my reddened cheeks under my best gown, I greeted Wulfgar at the door. The big warrior looked tired, lines of care falling away when he saw me approaching with a horn of mead. He took it silently and drank, his eyes never once leaving my form.

"Thank you," he said when the horn was empty. "How are you, Muriel?"

"Well, my lord." After my punishment, I felt it was best to stick to old formalities. I'd been on my best behavior with Fergus all afternoon. I made bread and meat stew, cleaned and swept the hearth, and shook out the pelts on the bed. The red-haired warrior had kissed me and left to take a patrol around the perimeter minutes before I heard Wulfgar's footfalls on the stoop.

"Something smells good."

"I made dinner." I backed away, putting the table between me and the giant warrior. The cabin seemed so much smaller with him inside. "It's simple fare. I can serve you, unless we should wait for Fergus."

"He is needed elsewhere." After barring the door, Wulfgar removed his weapon belt and leaned his ax against the wall, though he lay his short sword at the ready on the table.

"I heard about your little adventure today," he said as he sat.

"I'm sorry," I winced, wondering if he would add to my punishment, but he waved my worry away.

"I know you atoned for it. I hope your chastisement was enough to teach you to mind."

"It was, my lord."

"Good. It does not surprise me that there are wolves waiting in the forest for a glimpse of you. Probably one of Siebold's cronies, spying on you for him." He rubbed a hand over his face, the great slope of his shoulders sagging with weariness. "The pack is restless. That's why I was gone today. The Alpha's called me to discipline a few wayward wolves."

"Are you the only one who can bring order?" With nervous hands, I busied myself with the fire and soup pot. I'd grown used to having Fergus as a buffer between me and the powerful, scarred warrior. Wulfgar's size and forbidding looks still overwhelmed me.

"The Alphas have great power over the pack, but when that fails, it is good for them to have a third, strong fighter."

"The Alphas told me you were called 'the Enforcer.'"

"Aye, Muriel. That is what they call me." At his sad tone, I glanced back in shock.

"Did you...did you have to kill anyone today?" I couldn't help my voice quivering, but I tried my best to keep the censure out of my question.

"Not today. Not tomorrow, either, I hope. It all depends on how well the warriors keep their control."

"Are you ever in danger of losing control?"

"It has been many years since I have allowed my beast to rule." He added in a low murmur, almost too low for me to hear, "I fear the day when it will."

"I don't." I blurted before I could think. I bit my lip, but he was already waiting for me to explain.

"I mean, I still fear the power of the warrior who nearly killed Siebold. I am still learning who you are; the different parts of you, man, beast and wolf. From what I know so far, you'd never allow your beast to hurt anyone you care about. You'd find a way to make your own end before you did that."

He stared at me, and his gaze hit me like a blow. Whatever power Wulfgar had went beyond his great muscles and warrior skill. The magic in him gave him the ability to rule men with a look, a thought. Caught like a fish in the net, my eyes watered but I couldn't look away.

Finally he broke the silence. "I wish that were true. In the past, it has not been true. I've made mistakes." He seemed to want to continue, but bit off the rest of his comment with frustration. When he looked away, I hid my sigh of relief. "It will be good for the pack when your sister Fleur is mated off, but then we must find brides for the rest. To ask these warriors to go many more years unmated...it will be certain death. The beast will consume their minds. A shame to watch good men fall. Men who were once my friends."

As I served his plate, I took his hand in mine. Emboldened by our intimate conversation, I kissed the rough knuckles.

"All will be well, sir."

I dropped his hand and moved away before he could say or do anything more. Scurrying out of reach at the opposite side of the table, I watched him through a curtain of my hair. My massive warrior was not handsome but there was a sturdiness to his features that pleased me. The way he stared at me, I knew my form pleased him too.

He dipped bread into the broth and grunted his approval. "By the moon, it is good to come home to a warm hearth and a good meal."

"Does the pack not know how to cook stew?" I teased.

"We hunt and cook over the open flame. There's nothing like roast boar under a starry sky, but after a century or two it grows old."

Moving carefully because of the plug, I perched on the edge of the table opposite him. It put our heads at the same height, which gave me courage. "You could not build lodges and cabins for you to live in?"

"We dared not until your sisters came to us. In the past

the beast had taken over and destroyed all we built." He sighed. "No, Muriel, 'tis better for the Berserkers to live as beasts. No homes to welcome us. No women or friends to endanger. We make camp and cook like mercenaries, always ready to go into battle. Only the enemy is our own nature."

"A harsh life." It was my turn to sound sad.

"It is. I am glad to see the end of it. That is why I did all I could to win the Games." Raising his horn, he toasted me. After he drank he let the horn fall on his empty plate with a clatter. He drew off his jerkin and tossed it aside.

The sight of his muscles made my mouth water. I wanted to run my hands over them and explore the pebbled sheet of his stomach. My sex grew hot and wet thinking of touching him.

Wulfgar tilted his head and I knew he scented me.

"Come here, little one."

I went to stand between his two legs thick as tree trunks. As intimidating as he was, my heart beat faster when he put his hand on my hips and drew me even closer. "Do you know what I love more than the soft bed and hot stew? "

"What, my lord?"

"A beautiful woman. My woman."

"I'm sure my lord has enjoyed many women."

Pain flickered in his face, creasing his forehead along with his old scar, but before I could ask what unhappy thought marred his features, it was gone.

"I only have thoughts for the one who is in my arms." I flushed and turned my head so my hair fell over my face. Close as I was, I could not hide my eagerness from him.

"I hear Fergus has been at work preparing you for tonight."

"Yes."

"He plugged you, did he not?"

I nodded, too overcome to speak.

"Show me." His chair scraped back from the table as he gave me space to obey.

Embarrassed though I was, I dared not disobey. Turning, I drew up my dress and bent at my waist. I heard him suck in his breath at the sight of my plugged bottom. I bit my lip and waited.

When his touch came, it was the barest feather-light stroke of my lower lips. My knees grew weak. I trembled and would've fallen.

"Sit on my lap, little wife." I started to obey and he tugged my shift. "Lose this."

I drew it over my head. Standing bare before him, I tried not to feel nervous. I curled my hands into fists, resisting the urge to pull my hair over my flesh like a garment.

His eyes roamed up and down, the heat in his eyes setting fire to my blood.

"On my lap now." He helped me straddle him.

As soon as my wet heat touched his bare stomach, I gasped.

"Does it feel good?"

"Yes, sir."

His chuckle vibrated through him and did all sorts of wonderful things to me, inside and out. As my breathing sped up, his attention dropped to my bare breasts.

"These are lovely." His finger hovered an inch away from my areola.

"They are yours to touch whenever you please," I reminded him.

For a while he did just that, amusing himself. I settled further onto his carved stomach, pressing my slick heat onto the unyielding muscle.

Wulfgar thumbed a nipple and my hips jerked naturally, my center finding the contact it craved.

"That's it." Gold rose in his eyes. Was this Wulfgar the man or the beast? "Rock against me, take your pleasure."

He rolled my nipples between a large thumb and forefinger. Everything about us was so different. He was hard where I was soft, large where I was small, but the hunger in my body matched the glint in his eyes.

I rocked on him, closing my eyes at the sensation. My cunny pulsed and honey poured from my center, slickening his stomach and easing my way. Little tendrils of pleasure curled through me as I rocked.

"Yes," he murmured. "Use me for your pleasure." Reaching back, he took the plug and started to twist it, pushing and pulling until my body arched as if trying to escape the strange sensation. Arousal and embarrassment rushed through me all at once. Having my bottom filled made my cunny all the more hungry for cock.

"Oh, my lord—"

"Call me Wulfgar." Sharp teeth found my ear and nipped. Fluid rushed out of me. "You're going to cum for me, Muriel."

"I can't," I gasped. "Fergus said I must not cum until he allows it."

"Fergus is not your only master," Wulfgar growled. He removed the plug with a sudden pop. Cupping my bottom, he stood. My legs twined around his middle as he carried me to the bed. Once there, he turned and sat, still holding me on his lap.

He lay back, broad form stretching before me, an awe inspiring landscape of muscle for me to explore. I set my hand on his abdomen to steady myself, and his cock grew hard against my bottom.

"That's it, Muriel." He encouraged, and I needed no further encouragement. My small hands traced the peaks and valleys of his great chest, caressing the knotted muscle. One day I would be brave enough to kiss where my hands went, to map his beautiful body with my lips and tongue.

For now, Wulfgar had other plans.

"Up," he pulled me over him and set me right on his face. I gasped as I realized how he wanted me to straddle him. The stubble on his chin scratched my secret places and I rose up. Firm hands pulled me back down.

"Rock on my face. Ride me."

"Wulfgar," I gasped his name, then moaned as his mouth opened and hot air hit my womanly parts. My hips moved of their own volition, seeking the pleasure so recently denied. His tongue plunged into my channel and I threw back my head, riding faster, the wet warmth driving me wild.

My climax came suddenly, starting low in my belly and flashing through me. My back stiffened and my head snapped back as I bucked like a rider on a horse. Wulfgar's hands steadied and bit into my hips, holding me upright when I would've sagged down to the bed.

Finally he let me down and stretched over me. His face was wet.

"Muriel," he murmured my name over and over as he lay me down and took in my form, my chest flushed, my body soft and still quivering from his touch.

"Wulfgar." I reached for him, and he waited no longer.

He sank into me, my legs wrapped around his massive body as far as they would go.

"Please." I grasped at his heavily muscled arms and shoulders, enticing him closer. Finally I reached around and raked my nails down his back.

He howled and drove forward, slamming his cock into my channel again and again. The cabin filled with wet slapping sounds. My whole body bowed under his, my hips rising to meet his, little whispered pleas escaping my lips. My orgasm caught me and had me clenching around his cock, endless shockwaves carrying my pleasure on and on.

"Wulfgar, Wulfgar," I gasped, and a smile wreathed his face like dawn breaking through the clouds, the most beautiful sight I'd ever seen.

At last, he drove into me one final time, his heavy body pinning me as he grunted through his own climax. I stroked his strong shoulders, enjoying his weight on me. Safe, warm, protected in the shelter of his massive form, I gave him a happy half-lidded smile and traced his full lips where his own smile had been. He blinked at me in wonder, as if I was a creature sent from the goddess and he half expected me to disappear.

When he started to rise up, I caught his arm. "Please, stay here a little while."

I remembered too late that he preferred not to share my bed, that even during Fergus' and my lovemaking he kept his distance and took care not to touch me.

My happy feelings faded away. "It's all right if you do not wish to."

"I do wish to, Muriel," he said. "Am I hurting you?"

"No," he seemed to need more reassurance, so I wrapped my legs and arms around him again, and closed my eyes to focus on the sensation of his giant cock becoming soft inside me. He sank further onto me, arms coming to hold me as I held him. His beautiful lips nuzzled my neck.

"Tonight, we will mark you," he whispered in my ear. "You will be ours."

6

As the sun sank, Wulfgar and I went outside to wait for Fergus. My big mate gave me leave to roam around the clearing, as long as I didn't stray into the woods.

Spring had blossomed in the past week. The forest was filled with singing birds, new leaves, and flowers spreading their subtle scent on the wind.

In the twilight, Wulfgar took up his great axe and split wood. I sat on a stump and watched him as I worked on mending one of my gowns. The fluid motion of the muscles in his broad back made for a fascinating study. My cunny clenched at the sight, even though the memory of our love-making was so fresh, I could still feel the impression of him inside me, as if he'd marked me already.

I rose and returned to the cabin, checking the bread and moving the stew pot closer to the fire. I found myself pacing back and forth on the cabin porch, impatient for Fergus to return. Tonight the two of them would take me together in a final claiming. Even though evidence told me I wasn't a worthy mate, I had hope. Perhaps I would be pleasing enough that they would keep me longer.

An owl flew to a nearby branch. The broad span of its wings caught my eye and I turned, startled.

I was even more startled when the owl grew into a woman, with white blond hair and a beak-like nose. She was lovely, but her beauty was a hard shell around her.

Before I could shout for Wulfgar, or scuttle back into the cabin's relative safety, the lady said, "Well met, Muriel, mate of Fergus and Wulfgar."

My heart leapt, and I knew who my visitor was.

"Good evening, Yseult," I gave a little curtsy.

Her lips quirked.

"You know then that they are both my mates?"

"I do. She cocked her head. "I see the pack does not yet know they share you. Why do they hide you away?"

"They say we must work on our mate bond."

"And indeed you should, but there are many secrets being kept here."

I glanced at Wulfgar, but he didn't seem to notice the witch was here. Strange that he should be so unaware, but I guessed that whatever spell Yseult used to come to me, also kept our meeting private. "I did not wish to tell them I was worried, but they are worried too."

"Is that why you summoned me? You fear for your mating bond?"

"I fear the pack will try and test to see if my men are truly my mates."

Yseult watched me as unblinking as an owl. I tried to remember all Sabine had taught me about dealing with a witch. I must speak plainly and tell the truth, and ask specific questions. I blurted what I most feared, "Is it true that Siebold will try to claim me?"

"For a scrying, I need a payment. A boon."

For a moment my throat was too dry to speak. "Yes," I said, "anything I can give. Within reason." It wasn't wise to make open ended promises to a creature of magic.

"A lock of your hair."

"That is all?"

"A piece of yourself is not a trifle. It can be powerful, in the right hands. I will not use it for evil purpose, I assure you." Her eyes glittered. "At least, not this time."

My chest tightened as if my heart refused to beat, but I had already committed myself. Before I could think about it, I drew out my dirk and sliced off a shank of hair. "Is this enough?"

"Plenty."

I stretched out my hand, but Yseult didn't move. Instead, a raven flew down and snatched the offering from my fingers. I staggered back, clutching my hand to my breast while it flew up onto a nearby branch.

"Thank you, Muriel." Yseult smiled, a mirthless expression that looked like a mask on her face. "I cast the runes before I came here. Yes, you must bond, or others will seek to stake a claim on you. They will fight over your hand."

I RUBBED my hand where the raven's beak had stabbed it. "I do not wish for there to be more violence."

"There will be." Yseult's voice was low and mesmerizing. "Only you can stop it."

"How?"

She shrugged. "You become their mate."

"They are taking me, both together, tonight."

"That is a start. A very good start. Muriel, why do you wish to mate with them?"

I watched Wulfgar as he worked not two hundred steps away. The sweat on his hard muscled back shone in the dying light. "It is my duty."

"Only that?"

"I care for them."

"Even Wulfgar? The Pack Enforcer?"

"Yes."

"I will tell you that you must bond before the full moon, or they risk forfeiting you as their mate."

"Three days?" I could seduce them.

"Wait, did the runes say if it is possible for me to mate with them?"

Yseult cocked her head. "Do you know who you are?"

I twisted the cloth of my dress between my fingers. "I am Muriel of Alba."

"Daughter of a healer, who was daughter of a witch."

"My sister Sabine is the one with healing power."

"All four of you and your sisters are spaewives, a special race of women born with latent magic. Not quite witches, though you could become so. Your magic is natural, of the earth."

"I have no magic." The raven fluttered its wings on the branch above our heads, as if to contest my words. After all, I had done the spell to call Yseult, and she was here.

"You have powers, Muriel. I don't know what they will be, or if they will manifest. Your mother had great power, but she was afraid to use it. In the end, she shackled herself to a weak man and drank herself to death."

"She raised us."

"Aye. And now you must decide. Will you choose love, or fear?"

"I will do my duty." I said slowly.

"Then you've made your choice." Yseult dusted off her

shoulder, and the raven flew to her and landed there, dropping the shank of my hair into her hand. "To answer your question, you must mate with your two warriors, or others in the pack will try to kill them to lay claim to you."

My heart seized.

Yseult fixed me with a look. "Only you can stop this, Muriel. Use your powers. And one more thing." She lifted her hand to her mouth, hiding her pleased look. The next word I heard in an faint, echoing voice, spoken directly inside my head. *Don't ever give a witch a piece of your body. It allows them to control you.*

She was gone in a flash of light that made me jump. Not even the raven remained. Rubbing my eyes, I stumbled back inside the hut. From the sounds of chopping wood, Wulfgar was still at the chore. He hadn't noticed the witch's presence at all.

I decided there was no use worrying over what the witch had said about using my hair. There were many ways she could harm me, if she wanted to.

I also couldn't waste time wondering whether or not it was possible for me to be a Berserker bride. With three days, there was no time to waste. To force the bond and avoid being given back to the pack, I had to seduce my men.

Building up the fire, I crushed herbs and filled the hut with a sweet, heady smell. I laid out mead and meat on the table, and after I washed, I rubbed my skin with oil until it glowed.

Then I lay on the bed to await my warriors. I did not have to wait long. They came stomping in...and stopped in their tracks.

I smiled to myself. My naked body shone in the firelight, with only my long, brown hair as a covering. I'd faced away from the door, angling on my side so they could see my buttocks and trim waist, the curve of my back hinting at more alluring curves in front. With one leg propped up, I could easily slip my hand between my legs and touch myself. I did this now, readying my folds for my men.

"Getting started without us, lass?" I heard boots and clothes hit the floor.

"Mmhmm," I purred and looked over my shoulder at them. The past few days prepared me for the heart stopping sight of two large, muscled men making their way towards me, their intent gaze feasting on my flesh.

"Touching yourself is our right."

I rolled to my back. Both warrior's cocks jutted out in invitation. "Come, claim me, then."

They hastened forward.

"Naughty lass. You're not to touch yourself without our permission."

"Not even a little?" I asked with a sultry look as I lifted my hand and displayed the sticky wetness on my fingers. "I'm ready for you."

"Not quite." Fergus approached, holding up the plug. I rolled to my stomach with a mock groan. A hard smack on my bottom made me yelp.

"Come on, lass." Hands pulled me back into position, half on my belly and half on my side with several pelts bunched under me. Fergus spread oil between my cheeks before he replaced his fingers with the slick plug. "You'll be grateful ye were stretched when our cocks are inside ye."

I pouted, but grabbed one bottom cheek and lifted it for him to easily access my back hole. "You'll split me in two."

He grinned and twisted the plug inside

"Touch yourself while I fuck ye with it."

Biting my lip, I obeyed. Fergus gripped my bent leg,

holding me still as he pushed the wooden bulb into my forbidden orifice.

As the plug moved in and out, I kept my fingers fluttering against my sensitive spot. The dark sensation felt so wrong, yet my nipples beaded and the secret places between my legs tightened with anticipation.

I kept my gaze down, but could not keep the blush from spreading over my face.

"Do ye like it, Muriel?"

"No," I denied, but there was a catch in my voice.

Fergus chuckled softly. He loved to prove his power over me. "We'll teach ye to cum just from this. Don't stop touching, or you'll be cumming with a red bum."

With a growl, Fergus moved. He lifted me with ease and my legs wrapped around his hard body.

"Ride me." Fergus slapped my buttock, spurring me on. Again and again he smacked it.

I did as he ordered and gave him a show, letting my breasts bounce wildly as I canted my body up and down.

"Verrae nice," Fergus said. "But I want to see the plug." Grabbing my hips, he pulled me off his cock and turned me to straddle him facing his feet.

I sat still, confused, until he jerked his hips, impaling me again. This time, as he fucked me from below, he toyed with the plug, making me moan. I felt fuller than I ever had before, my insides deliciously stimulated.

"Soon Wulfgar and I will take ye like this, together."

Wulfgar approached the bed, pulling on his massive member. "We'll start now."

He knelt on the bed, and I leaned forward almost onto all fours and took Wulfgar into my mouth as I'd been taught. I moaned around him as Fergus filled me from below. The young warrior gripped my hips and thrust up so I bounced. Wulfgar steadied me.

"Try this." Fergus changed positions so he knelt behind me to plow me from behind. When he drove forward, I slid onto Wulfgar's cock, swallowing him further.

I choked.

"Not so hard, brother," Wulfgar cradled my jaw as I took a moment to cough.

"I can do it," I said when I'd caught my breath. "I'm ready." I opened my mouth wide, but Wulfgar waited until he was sure I could take him. Slowly he fed me his length, cupping either side of my head.

"Now, brother," Wulfgar gave the signal and they both started moving. Gently at first, pushing and thrusting at opposite times so I rocked between them.

My hands fisted on the pelts, body torn between focusing on pleasing Wulfgar with my mouth, and bouncing back onto Fergus' member.

"Relax, Muriel," Wulfgar murmured. "Let us use ye."

His big hand kneaded my shoulder, a thumb stroking my cheek. I stilled and let myself become a vessel for their cocks.

Their movements started slowly, falling into an easy rhythm. Every time Fergus pushed into my wet hole, I swallowed Wulfgar down further. Their grunts filled the cabin. I hummed around Wulfgar's cock and he cursed and sighed. His hands caught my jaw, cushioning my chin as he began to speed up his thrusts.

Fergus slammed into me harder and harder. Deep inside me, feelings of pleasure curled tighter and tighter, ready to snap. My body began to tremble.

"She is ready," Wulfgar rumbled above me. I looked up

and he'd grown a wicked set of canines, ready to bite my flesh. I'd wear the scar forever. "It is time."

They changed positions. Wulfgar lay on his back with his member standing ready. Fergus guided me to straddle the large warrior, then pushed me flush to his chest. Slick from my mouth, the giant cock slid into my cunny easily.

Wulfgar caught my chin. Tipping up my head, he kissed me long and hard. His tongue delved deep.

Behind me, Fergus removed the plug.

With his fingers he spread something slick around my back hole and stimulating and stretching me further while I moaned into Wulfgar's mouth. My bottom felt strangely empty.

"Perfect," Fergus announced. With two firm hands holding my bottom cheeks apart, he set his cock at my back channel, and pushed in.

"Oh, please, oh please," I gasped. Wulfgar's great girth and Fergus' length pressed into my very mind, driving every thought from my head but the sensation of their cocks invading my body. I shook between them.

"Shhh," Wulfgar soothed, even as Fergus cursed above me.

"By the moon, Muriel. You're the goddess incarnate."

I pressed my forehead to Wulfgar's neck, quivering. My men had me sandwiched between them, impaled on their cocks. I could barely move, much less think.

"Are you alright, sweetheart?" Wulfgar petted my hair and used it to draw my head back to look at him.

"Mmm," I replied. His face creased into a smile.

I blinked a few times before I found my voice. "Now what?"

"Now," he tucked my head back against the bunched muscles of his shoulder. His lips found my ear while his large arms wrapped around me to steady me further. "We fuck you."

His hips started moving, scything in and out of my cunny. Fluids dripped.

Above me, Fergus gripped my waist and began gliding in and out of me, too.

Closing my eyes, I clutched at Wulfgar. All I could do was hold on and remember to breathe as my men used me for our pleasure.

They rocked me between them, and set my whole body to singing.

My climax blew through me and kept going, an endless undulation. Pleasure kept rising, rising inside me, only to drop me from a great height, where I shattered. Just as I recovered, the sensations began to mount up again. Sounds escaped my throat, incoherent pants and moans that seemed to drive my men into a frenzy.

Fergus thrust into me harder and harder, his hips slapping into my bottom. Wulfgar tugged my hair, wrenching my head sideways. He set his teeth to my shoulder and the sting pierced my happy haze.

"Yes," I sobbed. "Hurt me. I'm yours."

The teeth withdrew, and I missed the pain that eased the sharp edge of pleasure. My body was overcome.

I squeezed my holes tight, hard, and Fergus came, bucking over me. Wulfgar's grunts told me he'd climaxed as well.

Body still humming, I waited, limp on my lover's broad body, but the teeth did not pierce my skin.

Fergus kissed my back, and both bottom cheeks, tickling me with his stubbled face before collapsing next to us on the bed.

His hand found mine and twined in it. Warmth flooded through me.

"But what about the bond?" I tried to ask, but my words came out an unintelligible mumble.

A rumbling chuckle shook me. Wulfgar pushed my hair from my back and stroked my skin with his rough hands.

"Sleep, little one."

I mumbled again, but his voice and soothing touches were as potent as a long, drugging draught, and I slept.

FREEZING air gusted over my face and I twitched.

"Cold," I grunted.

"Stay in bed, little one. Fergus will be back soon. It was his turn to get the wood."

Wulfgar bent over me to tuck a great fur robe around me before reseating himself by the fire.

I bit my lip, and didn't ask why he would avoid my bed.

Soreness lingered in my cunny, a pleasant reminder of the night's events. My men had taken me completely. Yseult would approve.

Yet they still had not giving me claiming marks. I touched my shoulders and frowned.

Wulfgar had come so close to marking me, and then drawn back. Why? What had I done wrong?

Shadows played over the great warrior's face as he drank from a horn and watched the fire.

Fergus came in, his breath like smoke.

"It's coming down hard out there." He dusted white powder off his shoulders and stomped his feet. "I stacked more wood on the porch, out of the flurries."

"Snow in springtime?" I sat up and pulled the bear robe

around my shoulder. The red points of Fergus' cheeks and nose made me shiver in sympathy.

"There have been flurries late as summer in this part of the world." Wulfgar handed his warrior brother the drinking horn.

"This isnae just snow, it is a blizzard," Fergus said once. "I scented something strange on the wind earlier when I was returning home. It must have been the winter wind, pushing in."

I shivered again. Yseult had visited late afternoon. Had Fergus scented her? Had her magical presence disturbed the weather?

"Cold, sweetling?" Fergus came to me, rubbing his hands together. "I can think of a way to warm ye up."

"Fergus, no, you have snow on you—"

The young warrior stopped and stripped off his clothes. In a flash, he'd turned into the red wolf. One hard shake sent the rest of the melting flakes flying. They sizzled on the hearth, and Fergus leapt onto the bed. Tongue lolling out, he lay half on me.

"You're wet," I protested. "And heavy."

He licked my face and I sputtered. After a minute, I had to admit his weight and heavy fur coat did warm me.

Wulfgar sat watching us with a small smile.

"Come to bed?" I invited.

He shook his head. "I must patrol."

"Surely the snow will keep our enemies away."

"That is not why I patrol, Muriel. My beast does not like confined spaces."

"But-" I looked to Fergus for help, but he just gave me sad wolf eyes, and sighed.

Wulfgar hefted the great axe and slipped out the door, leaving me trapped under a giant, sleeping wolf.

I SLEPT FITFULLY, hearing echoes of my men's voices in my dreams, though Wulfgar was gone all night, and Fergus was in wolf form.

"The bond, do you feel it?"

'Not yet, Little Red."

"I thought it would form when we took her together."

"Perhaps after a few nights. It will soon."

I woke with newfound determination to form the bond.

Fergus had Changed into a man as he'd slept. As usual, he woke hungry.

"Mmm," he nuzzled my neck.

"Fergus, that tickles."

His teeth grazed my shoulders and I closed my eyes.

The door slammed and Wulfgar loomed over us.

"None of that, brother," Wulfgar growled to Fergus.

With his elongated canines, Fergus' teeth looked wicked. "I was just going to take a wee bite."

"Not yet," Wulfgar said.

I sighed and sagged back onto the bed. I had to win over my giant mate.

"Is the blizzard over?" Fergus asked as Wulfgar crouched at the fire.

"Ended late last night. There's a snow up to a rabbit's ear, but the day is already warming. By noon it will be mostly melted away."

"Odd weather," Fergus said, and Wulfgar grunted his agreement.

"If the river swells, we may have to leave the cabin, seek higher ground."

"It'll be time to return to the pack, soon." Fergus glanced at me, tellingly.

I resisted the urge to cover my shoulders. A night of fucking and I was still unmarked. What would the pack say? My sisters and everyone would know I'd failed as a Berserker bride.

"Seeing as we're snowed in..." Fergus grabbed the robe covering me and pulled it off. I shrieked, grabbing at it to cover my nude form.

"Fergus, it's cold!"

"Well," he held the robe out of reach. "What will ye give me for it?"

"A kiss." I pouted.

"Verrae well. Come kiss me, then."

Diving back under the proffered covers, I wriggled up to face Fergus.

"Good morning," I smiled, twining my arms around his neck.

"Good morning, lass," he said and kissed me.

I broke away and reached out to Wulfgar. "Come lie with us," I invited.

He smiled and stood. I kept my hand outstretched as he stretched and stripped off his boots and clothes.

Meanwhile Fergus was kissing down my neck. I rolled away from him, arms crossed over my breasts.

"I'm not your mate yet, am I?"

"You're whatever we say ye are."

"Fergus," I started to protest, but I couldn't argue with his fervent kisses, pressed down the curve of my spine. His small beard tickled me and made me shiver, ready for kisses in another place.

As if he knew my thoughts, he grabbed my leg and flipped me over.

"I know what I want to eat for breakfast."

"Fergus, no...I have not bathed." My men had cleaned

me up as best they could, but my own juices mingled with their seed.

"Ye smell like us," Fergus' stubble scraped my bottom. His teeth nipped me and I yelped.

Wulfgar sat and I scrambled to him, crawling onto his lap.

He did not smile outright but his eyes crinkled and he helped me straddle him.

I smoothed my hands down his great shoulders, squeezing the granite muscles. His size and masculine scent made my insides quiver. "What do you want to do this morning?"

The big warrior took a fistful of my hair and clenched it thoughtfully. "You." With one hand in my hair and one steadying my hip, he thrust up inside me.

My head fell back, my nails digging into his arms for purchase. Drawing me closer, he nuzzled my neck. Wet and ready, my cunny tightened around him as I waited for him to claim me.

"Mark me," I whispered. "please."

Desire flickered across his face, followed by concern. "Not yet."

"Please. I want it. We must bond."

His hips jerked once, twice, and then he lifted me off his cock and set me away.

Fergus caught my hair and used it as a leash to pull me to him.

"Are ye thinking of the bond and not pleasing us? Naughty lass." I found myself over his lap. He spanked my bottom until I squealed. None of the slaps truly hurt, and my cunny dripped all down his leg.

Pausing, he checked between my legs. "Soaking wet.

This willnae teach ye to mind. We'll have to think up a worse punishment."

"Do it," Wulfgar growled.

With a hard fist in my hair, Fergus drew my head back. His other hand cradled my throat "Would ye like that, Muriel? I can give ye a taste of the whip. It has a wee bite, but can also give ye pleasure."

My eyes were heavy lidded, my body flooded with desire. "Yes, please. Whip me, mark me, make me yours."

In my mind's eye I saw myself stretched out before them. Using a whip made of soft strands of deerskin with one end bound into a handle Fergus flogged my front and back until my skin was red and striped. At the erotic image my body shook with overwhelming pleasure.

I came, panting and gasping.

"Naughty one. Ye do not deserve our cocks."

"Please," I said. Crouching on all fours, I raised my bottom and lowered my head, offering myself like a bitch in heat.

When I glanced back, both my mates had eyes of bright gold.

Then Wulfgar shook his head.

"Finish her, Fergus," he said. "I must go. The Alphas are calling me."

He walked out.

I broke my position, dashing tears from my ears.

"Lass, why are ye crying?"

"I want him. I do. I want to bond with both of you."

"Ye will, sweet one. Why do ye not trust us?"

"Because it hasn't happened yet. What if it never will?"

"Hush, lass. You worry so."

The witch's warning was on the tip of my tongue, but I

bit it back. "What if I can't bond with you? I'm afraid. I'm not like Brenna or Sabine."

"Your submissive nature makes ye a perfect bride for us. Ye are so, so good, but afraid. We hope, in time, to break through your shell and let the real Muriel out."

"I am the real Muriel." I huffed.

"Don't pout, sweetling," Fergus tugged my hair. "All this thinking about the bond isnae good for ye. The bond forms here," he laid a hand over my heart, right where the ache was. "When the time is right, ye will feel it."

Unless I couldn't bond at all. I shook him off so I wouldn't cry. "The morning grows old. May I go outside today?"

"Aye, lass. It's warm enough now I can take ye."

Outside, a group of trees had exploded into white blossoms, as if to celebrate the passing of the bizarre snowstorm. I plucked the branches to make a floral wreath while Fergus romped in wolf form among the mud puddles.

He came to me, fur wet and filthy, and I backed away.

"No, no. I don't want to get dirty. And you better wash in the stream before you go in the cabin," I scolded before turning back to my flowers.

Wee Muriel. Always doing her duty.

I whirled, but there was only the red wolf, panting happily. Yet I'd heard Fergus' voice clear as day.

Perhaps the witch's magic still lingered, or I'd grown as fey as Fleur, to be hearing things no one said.

I'd finished a wreath, and started another that I'd make Fergus' wolf wear around his neck, a threat I'd made to keep his muddy paws away from my gown, when the bushes shook. A flash of white, and I staggered back just in time to avoid a giant wolf toppling me over.

"Fergus," I screamed. With a gust of magic, the white

wolf grew into a Berserker warrior with heavy brows and a shock of white running through his otherwise dark hair.

Fergus jerked me back, putting himself between me and the intruder.

A second wolf joined the first, and transformed into a warrior with the same gust of wind and a stomach-churning crackle of shifting skin and bone. The two were naked but for a loincloth, and a wolf pelt slung across their shoulders. Their eyes glowed, but they didn't advance. As we waited, the bushes behind them rippled in advent of a third wolf.

"Muriel, quickly, go inside and bar the door. Ye must not come out," Fergus whispered.

"What is this? Are they from your pack?"

"Never you mind that. Stay inside, they will not hurt ye."

The two waiting warriors stayed silent. A rush of wind lifted the edge of my skirts, and Siebold strode from the forest. Other than a bright red scar slashing across his chest, the blond had healed from his grievous battle wounds.

Only two days, and he had come for me. The witch was wrong.

"Muriel, inside now."

"No, Fergus, he's here for me." I grasped his arm. "They will hurt you."

"Muriel," he bit out, "Listen to me."

"Well, if it isn't the runt. Where's the Enforcer?"

Smirking, Siebold stepped closer and snatched up a wreath I'd left on the ground.

Naked but for a loincloth, Fergus kept himself between the blond and me.

"Wulfgar set me as guard. He's on the hunt."

"He better take care his little bitch doesn't wander off. Otherwise another wolf might snatch her."

"Muriel, for the last time, go inside," Fergus ground out.

"No, I won't leave you." I hovered at his back. Wulfgar, please come. I prayed.

"How is it lying with the Enforcer? Has he broken you yet?"

"Don't answer," Fergus ordered. "Ye cannot speak directly to him unless Wulfgar is here."

"Do you know what Wulfgar did to the last woman who lay with him?" Siebold and the other three fanned out, circling now, trying to find an in. "Shall I tell you, Muriel? Are you brave enough to hear the truth about your intended mate?"

"Don't listen to him," Fergus said, and my fingers tightened on his arm.

" You're paired with a wolf who kills his lovers. The last time Wulfgar lay with a woman, he lost control of his beast and snapped her neck. You should beg me to appeal to the Alphas. If you're lucky, they will listen, and give you to me."

"I'd rather die than be with you, Siebold," I snapped back, ignoring Fergus' warning. "Wulfgar is ten times the warrior that you are."

Siebold snarled.

Fergus snarled back.

"Enough!" with a roar and rush of power that blew my hair back, Wulfgar strode into the clearing. Ignoring the interlopers, he caught my eye and jerked his head towards our dwelling. "Into the hut, Muriel. Now."

I raised my skirts and ran. Fergus followed, stopping halfway between the cabin and the enemy warriors. Slipping inside, I kept the door open a crack.

Siebold and his cronies now circled Wulfgar. The giant warrior stayed planted in one spot. With a yawn, he stretched, his neck cracking as if with the Change. "Come to challenge me again? The beating in front of the entire pack wasn't enough to suit you?"

Fur sprouted along Siebold's arms as his beast gained control, but his face remained a man's. "I caught your mate sneaking around without you. She was dallying with the runt. If you can't even bring her to heel. Why should you be her mate?"

"My mate spends time with who I allow," Wulfgar answered. He looked perfectly at ease, hands at his sides, body poised on the balls of his feet.

"You let him near her? If you share her with the runt, perhaps you will share her with the rest of the pack."

Before Siebold stopped talking, he darted forward. Wulfgar growled, a low chilling sound that unraveled my spine.

Siebold halted.

Wulfgar pointed to him. "You will say away from here. Upon the pain of death. The Alphas will allow me to kill you for trespassing on my territory and threatening my mate."

"This isn't over," he spat. Signalling his silent cronies, he stalked off.

Just like that it was over.

I pulled back from the door, wiping my sweaty palms on my dress.

Fergus came into the hut first, and advanced on me, golden eyes burning.

"I told ye to go inside. Why did ye not do as I say?"

"They would've hurt you. I could not let that happen."

With a mighty kick, he sent the water bucket crashing into the wall. I jumped. "It is not your duty to keep me from fighting Siebold. I am supposed to be the one to protect ye."

"But you're not strong enough," I said. "Siebold is bigger

and he hates you. He wants to kill you. Don't you see? I can't let that happen."

Fergus' face turned red. I bit my tongue, wishing I could take my words back.

The door almost came off its hinges as Wulfgar pulled it open and walked in, gold eyes wild. He pointed at me. "Next time Fergus commands you inside, you go, immediately. Understand?"

"A good strapping will make her obey," Fergus grunted.

I crossed my arms over my chest. "Punish me. Spank me, even strap me. I only wanted to see you safe."

"So now ye are going to fight my battles for me?" Fergus asked.

I turned to Wulfgar. "Siebold accused me of dallying with Fergus behind your back. I had to do something."

"You should've obeyed," Wulfgar said quietly. He remained near the door, his body edged with tension. "Fergus can handle Siebold. You cannot."

"Why was Siebold going to tell the pack I was unfaithful to you? Don't they know you and Fergus share a brother bond?" A guilty look and the truth came to me. "They don't, do they. The pack doesn't know you two are bonded. That's why no one warned me that I would end up with two mates." I turned to Wulfgar. "They knew you'd win. Wulfgar the great warrior, the Enforcer. None could stand against you. No one knew I'd end up with two mates instead of one."

I swiveled to face Fergus. "You befriended me. You seduced me from the start. Why did you not tell me of your bond?"

"It had to be a secret."

"We should've told you, confided in you," Wulfgar said.

"Under normal circumstances, we could've wooed and courted you."

"But we could not," Fergus said. "Please understand. I wanted to tell ye, but finding a way to be with ye was more important.

"More important than telling me the truth?"

His chin jutted out. "The games were our best chance, and keeping our bond hidden gives us an edge."

"It hurts you," I said, bluntly. "You would be stronger if you were not keeping your bond a secret from the pack."

Wulfgar's brow creased. "Perhaps. But we will keep it between us for now."

"What makes ye say that, Muriel?" Fergus asked.

"I don't know. Never mind," I passed a hand over my face, wishing I could wipe the events of the day away as easily. "I wish I had known sooner. I could've chosen you."

"What?" my two warriors spoke together.

"At the very end, the Alphas gave me a choice. I thought it would throw the pack into chaos. I did not take my chance. If I had known, I could've chosen the two of you, and Siebold might not be up to these tricks."

"We did what we thought best," Wulfgar said in a low voice.

"And I do my duty," I tried, and failed, to keep bitterness from my tone. The cabin was suddenly too small for the three of us. I went to stand before the fire and stare into the flames.

Never mind that they hadn't trusted me. Never mind that my fate had rested in the hands of men I barely knew, and they wouldn't let me help them, because they thought I couldn't. Sabine and Brenna were lauded in the packs for their courage and strength. With each day that passed, it became more clear I was not fit to be a Berserker mate.

"This is wrong," I said bluntly. "You kept this from the pack, but you also kept it from me. Mates don't keep secrets. Not because they don't want to, but because they can't. You can speak mind to mind, can't you?"

"I get thoughts, impressions of feelings," Wulfgar said. "When he wishes, I hear his voice echo in my head. Not everything. But most things can be shared, yes."

"You need to trust me," I said. "If you truly believe I have courage enough to be yours, then you will treat me as an equal. Protect me where I am weaker, but trust me and confide in me, as you ask me to trust you."

"You are right, Muriel." Wulfgar's soft tone told me his beast had receded. "You humble us, and we beg your forgiveness."

Wulfgar came to my side, and I angled my body so I face both my men. "Granted."

"We have waited so long for a mate, we are still learning what that means," Fergus added.

"I love you. I have loved few things in my life, because it was safer to be sheltered." In my heart I prayed it would be enough. "I fear my love will not be enough. I must bond to you, or Siebold will challenge again for me."

"Who told you that?"

I hesitated before admitting, "The witch."

"The witch?" Wulfgar pushed forward, growling, "I thought I smelled her and her ilk." His hands searched me. Cupping my chin and angling my head, running down my arms and torso, he made sure there were no marks. "Did she come close? Did she touch you?"

"Why would she appear? Does she mean harm?" Fergus asked Wulfgar, who grunted.

I brushed Wulfgar's concerned hands away. "No, she does not mean harm. I summoned her."

Silence and all the air left the room.

"It was simple. Sabine taught me the spell. I was worried that I did not have any magic, but when I did the ritual, Yseult came."

I could barely meet my warrior's aghast looks.

"Why would ye do that?"

"I wanted to know what I must do to bond with you." I wrapped my arms around myself. My insides felt miserable. "I thought she could scry and tell me the outcome of our mating."

"Muriel," Wulfgar gripped my shoulders again, carefully. "What did you trade her for this knowledge?"

"A lock of my hair. It seemed a small price."

The giant heaved a sigh, and closed his eyes.

"I'm sorry. I wouldn't have done it if I had not been afraid."

"Muriel," Fergus shook his head. "Ye put yourself in danger. Went behind our backs—"

"I must bond with you," I cried. "I only have until the full moon. The runes say that Siebold will challenge you for me, Fergus. He can make a case that you didn't win me, only Wulfgar did. He will fight you and he will kill you."

"Are ye so sure? Ye do not think I even stand a chance in that fight?"

"Fergus," I held my hands out, a silent plea. "If you could have faced him, and won, why didn't you in the Games?"

I couldn't have struck a harder blow with my fists. Fergus faced me, his expression wild. "Ye don't think I'm good enough. Ye don't believe I am worthy of being your mate."

Mouth gaping, I looked to Wulfgar for help.

"No, Fergus, it is you who don't think that you are strong enough to deserve Muriel," the big warrior said softly.

"Maybe I'm not. But I'd like to at least have the chance to

prove myself." Fergus cursed. "Secrets and lies and lack of trust. Is it any wonder why we cannot bond?"

I wrung my hands. "Please, stop. I don't— you're twisting my words. It's my fault we have not bonded."

"It's not only on ye," Fergus said. "Ye take too much on yourself, Muriel."

"It's my duty."

"Duty," he spat. "Perhaps the beast would have ye mate with us out of love, not duty."

"You shouldn't have gone behind our backs, Muriel. We need you to trust us," Wulfgar said.

I looked from warrior to warrior. "Punish me, then. There is much I have to atone for."

"It is not so simple. Trust isnae so easily regained." Fergus shook his head and walked away.

I followed. "Please, don't leave me. I was trying to be brave, to be good. I was trying to protect you!"

He whirled on me to give a final parting shot, "Ye take my honor from me, Muriel. Ye should've left well enough alone." As he left, he slammed the door.

7

Wulfgar brushed by me and crouched near the hearth to feed more logs to the blaze. He kept his back towards me, his broad shoulders tense as if waiting for a blow.

When he rose, dusting off his hands, I ventured to ask, "Are you leaving me?"

"No. You are not to be left alone again."

"You can trust me."

He didn't answer, but grabbed a hunk of bread and a jug of mead, and started to leave. "Good night. If you need me, I'll be on the porch."

"Please come to bed," I begged. "Please, hold me."

"No, little one. I dare not."

"Is this because of what I've done?"

"No." He sounded defeated.

"Is it because...you're afraid you would hurt me?" No answer. "It's true, then, what Siebold said? You killed the last woman to share your bed."

"This is not something I wish to discuss with you."

"Please," I said, even as cold dread turned my stomach to stone. "Let there be no more secrets between us. "

"Very well," he sighed. "It's true. I loved a woman, we lay together, and one morning I woke up beside her and she was dead. Siebold knows because he found us."

I gasped and covered my mouth. "Tell me it's not true."

"I would that it weren't."

"I worked so hard not to give you a cause to fear me, but perhaps this is what the beast wants. Your fear, and obedience." His fingers traced my features and dropped to circle my throat.

I held still, pulse pounding against his palm

His grip loosened and dropped away. "No." Turned away.

"I hoped we would bond and the beast's cravings would die away. But they still beat at me."

"Stay with me. I want to help." I stretched out my arms.

"You should not trust me. I do not trust myself."

"Please."

"No. Say nothing more, Muriel. I am done for the night. I am done." He paused at the door and spoke over his shoulder. "Get some sleep. I'll stand watch, outside."

The door creaked shut after him.

I lay in bed, too stunned to cry. A week and I'd splintered my mates. Wulfgar and I hadn't overcome our fears. And Fergus, my first love, couldn't even look at me. What had I done?

As dawn approached, I took a fur robe and lay before the dying fire, too tired to build it up. Today I would make the journey to the pack. Fergus and Wulfgar deserved happiness. I would release them. I would go to the Alphas and tell them to cast me aside, or give me to Siebold, for I would never be good enough to be a Berserker mate.

Fergus found me in front of the charred logs, clutching a

wolf pelt to my chest. He had dark shadows under his eyes, and looked as bad as I felt.

I wanted to rise, to go to him, but would not be able to bear his rejection. Instead, I asked, "Where is Wulfgar?

"I came to ask ye the same thing. I cannot reach him."

My head throbbed as if someone had struck it. My hand went to my temple, and Fergus mirrored my action. The pain intensified and I let out a cry, wincing.

"Something is wrong. We must go to the Alphas."

"No, we cannot. Siebold waits there for us. He will challenge you for me."

"We have no choice. If Wulfgar and I are separated, I soon will be weakened." He held out his hand, no quarter in his tone. "Come Muriel. Ye will obey me."

With a prayer to the goddess, I went along. The minute our hands touched, some of the pain eased in my chest. Though he didn't speak, his fingers curled around mine, warming them, and I knew he felt the same. We walked in silence back to the mountain where the pack made their home.

THE HIGHER WE CLIMBED, the more Berserkers we saw. Most were in wolf form, stalking us slowly under the forest cover. Eventually we broke above the treeline and came into a clearing in front of a large cave. Samuel, the Highland Pack Alpha, sat in a seat carved out of the stone, overlooking a great bonfire. More wolves lounged there, in the shelter of the giant rocks thronging the wild, empty space.

Two guards rose as we approached, and I ducked my head against their hot gold gaze as Fergus led me between them.

"Here are the lovers." Siebold stood up from his place at the fire.

Samuel also rose from his throne. "Fergus, what is the meaning of this? Unhand Muriel."

"Muriel, come to me," Daegan ordered, but I ignored him, and stepped closer to Fergus.

"DO YOU SEE THIS INFIDELITY?" Siebold called out "I was telling the truth. Where is Wulfgar? She was given to the victor of the Games. Why does she come with Fergus?"

"Wulfgar and I share a bond," Fergus' voice rang out over the clearing,

I squeezed his hand harder.

A murmur ran around the pack, and from his throne like perch, Samuel leaned forward.

"A brother bond? How can this be?"

"As you know, I became a Berserker when Wulfgar rescued me. Since then the bond formed as we've saved each other's life."

Siebold scoffed. "If this is true, then you've kept this secret from the pack a long time. We need to call Wulfgar here to confirm it. If you are bonded to him, then call him and he will come."

"Wulfgar has been attacked. Injured. We came to get aid for him."

"Lies. If Wulfgar is hurt, it is because you and the prize conspired together to kill him."

Fergus met Siebold's gaze boldly. "So that's your game. If ye wish to fight me for Muriel, just challenge me, Siebold, and I will beat ye. Ye need not sneak around like a rabbit, finding ways for the Alphas to force us into a match."

Siebold swung his axe up and started forward, stopped only by Daegan's hand in his chest.

"Wait," Samuel ordered. "There will be no fights for dominance until I am satisfied. Fergus, is there proof of this brother bond?"

"It's true," I blurted. "I can vouch for their bond. They share everything, including me."

"A Berserker would not share his woman with any other, not unless he had a brother bond," Daegan confirmed.

"She lies for him," Siebold snarled. "She should be punished. Mates must be faithful to each other to keep order in the pack. Alpha, she must be whipped."

"Silence," Samuel thundered. "Fergus, call on Wulfgar via your bond. If he comes, we know you speak truth. If not, Muriel will be punished, and your life may be forfeit."

All the wolves settled down, but for the two guards at our back. The clearing quieted until the wind moaning past the stones was the only sound.

Sweat beaded on Fergus' forehead. "Alpha, I have called Wulfgar. As I said, something is wrong. He is unconscious, and may be wounded."

"I'VE REACHED out to him, also," Samuel said. "If he is injured, he can call on the power of the pack bonds to heal him faster."

"Alpha, if he was ambushed, his beast might have taken control," Fergus said. "I tell ye this so his lack of control does not infect the pack."

"If you are mated to Muriel, why isn't his beast under control?"

Staring at the ground, I bit my lip until I tasted blood.

Fergus answered, "We have not yet formed a mating bond with her."

"Siebold has a right to challenge you for her. Even if Wulfgar has won her hand, you have not. But the fact that you have not formed a bond is unsettling."

"It's my fault," I whispered, almost too low to hear, but in the stillness of the clearing, every wolf pricked up their ears. "I do not have the powers my sisters have. I am unable to bond."

"Muriel," Fergus murmured.

Tugging on his hand, I faced him and raised my voice louder. "But I love them. I choose them." I touched his face, tracing the freckles on his cheek, the stubble roughened line of his jaw. Tears tracked down my cheeks. "I'm sorry."

"It's alright, lass," he pulled me into his arms, where I sobbed.

"How long will you allow this infidelity to occur?"

"Shut up," Daegan said, even as Samuel gave the order. "Separate them. Her distress is affecting the pack. They want to go to war for you, Muriel, and they know not who to fight." He had no censor in his tone, but my gut twisted with it all the same.

Firm hands grabbed my arms, pulling me from Fergus.

"No," I tried to struggle against the guards, but they were too strong.

"Do not touch her," Fergus came alive, snapping an elbow back into one warrior's face. More Berserkers rushed to subdue him and I screamed as Fergus disappeared under a tangle of bodies.

"Stop!" Samuel's voice rang out. "Stop fighting or I cannot protect you."

"Enough," a familiar voice roared. Wulfgar limped into the clearing.

I stomped on the surprised guard's foot, and broke free to run to him.

The giant warrior was covered in dirt and blood. One eye was swollen and his whole head looked bruised. His right arm hung crookedly, but he reached out his other and brought me close to his side. I clutched at his torn jerkin as the Alphas questioned him.

"Wulfgar? What has happened to you?"

"Ambush. Wolves attacked me and threw me in the quarry while I was on my way back to my brother and my mate." He touched his head with a wince. "I woke and got halfway up the mountain before the ringing in my head stopped long enough for me to hear the pack bonds." He frowned, running a hand down my back. "What wolves have been touching my mate?" When he raised his head to glare at the pack, a few warriors shuffled backwards.

"Who attacked you?" Daegan asked. He stood between Siebold and Fergus. The latter had two wolves holding his arms, and a third with a blade at his neck.

"I did not see. They covered my head with a sack first. No doubt someone who wants to take my mate from me and my warrior brother." He gave Fergus a grim nod and a sigh seemed to go through the pack.

"Release him," Samuel ordered the wolves holding Fergus.

Wulfgar turned me to face him. "Little one, why were you crying?"

"I am not worthy to be your mate. Forgive me."

He sighed. "There is nothing to forgive." With a crack of newly grown bone, he settled his formerly hurt arm around my shoulders. Already his eye looked better.

"This doesn't settle my challenge, Alphas," Siebold was shouting. "I demand a new contest. Wulfgar won Muriel, but not Fergus. The runt must prove his strength if he is to claim her."

"Come fight me then," Fergus threw out his hands in challenge, but Samuel growled for silence.

"Peace. Wulfgar, do you accept Muriel as your given mate?"

"I do," Wulfgar rumbled.

"Wulfgar," I clutched at him. "You should not keep me. You can take my sister or another who can bond--"

"Hush, little one. There was never any question whether I would keep you.' He caught my chin. "I would fight in the Games all day, sleep and rise to do it all over again, if only to spend the nights with you."

I rested my head against him. He kept his hand on my hair as he announced, "Muriel is mine by right. Fergus and I share a brother bond, and we both claim her."

"I'll fight to defend my right to her," Fergus added.

I stiffened. "Wulfgar, no, you must stop it--"

"Hush, Muriel. Trust your mates."

Siebold was stalking around the bonfire, swinging his axe. "Are you sure, runt? I am one of the greatest warriors in the pack and you are the least."

"I'm sure," Fergus said, and spat on the ground. "Ye were never the greatest, Siebold. Ye only think ye are."

"Fergus, you've challenged Siebold for dominance," Samuel said. "The fight will take place tomorrow in front of the entire pack. If you win, your reward is Muriel."

"And if he loses?" I asked Wulfgar in a horrified whisper. "Will I go to Siebold?"

"Never. I will keep you."

"What happens to Fergus?" Siebold still stalked around the fire, throwing taunts at the silent redhead.

"Siebold will not show mercy, as I showed him. Fergus cannot lose."

8

W e arrived back at the cabin at dusk. Wulfgar carried me, though I protested when he'd swung me into his arms.

"You are hurt."

"I am not so weak that I cannot carry you. It does the pack good to see that I am able to care for my mate," he'd told me, but as soon as he set me on my feet inside the door, I ran for my herbs and bandages.

"How many attacked ye?" Fergus asked in a grim tone.

"Six," Wulfgar sucked in a breath as I pulled a broken claw from his back. "All from our pack."

"The cowards could not challenge ye for dominance, so they jumped ye alone."

"This is madness," I dabbed at the wound, but it was already closing. "The Games were supposed to stop the fighting."

"We will never stop fighting for ye, Muriel," Fergus sat in the chair balanced on its back two legs, his arms crossed in front of him.

"You should not." I swallowed hard. "I could go to Siebold and tell him—"

Both my warriors were on their feet, growling.

I backed away, twisting my hands. "Please, I want to help. I would do anything to save your life, my love," I pleaded with Fergus, whose face was stone.

"Even give yourself to a warrior who will be cruel to ye? Who will mistreat ye?"

"Answer him, Muriel," Wulfgar said.

"He will kill you," I pleaded with Fergus.

"And so ye will agree to be his mate? Did ye not think that he would have to kill us anyway, before we would allow him to take ye?"

"Please," I begged.

"Enough," Wulfgar said. "Enough of this fighting between us."

I gulped down my anguish. We had only one night to be together.

"We must work on our mate bond," Wulfgar continued.

"There is a matter of her punishment," Fergus said. I could tell by his look he hadn't forgiven me for doubting his ability to fight.

Wulfgar lifted my hair from my shoulders and pressed his lips to my neck. He wrapped his arms around me and I felt his touch was the only thing holding me together.

"I'm sorry," I said in a watery whisper. "Please whip me. I deserve it."

"Yes, we will punish you, but not in the way you think. No whippings, no punishment in front of the pack. This is between us, and you will remember this night and who you belong to forever. Now, Muriel, no more tears." Wulfgar wiped my face with the bandages that I would have used to bind his wounds.

I picked the cloth from his hands. "I need these for you."

He released me and showed me his blood-streaked body. His skin was unbroken.

"They are already healed. My magic is strong. We are stronger than you know. And there is a bond between us. You must trust it, Muriel. Trust your mates, but, most of all, trust yourself. Can you do that?"

"I can try."

"Good girl," he said and I melted a little. He cuddled me closer and kissed my forehead. Fergus still stood with his back to us, frustration in the set of his shoulders.

"Fergus," Wulfgar called. "She needs to know that you forgive her."

With a sigh, my red-headed warrior turned. "Come here, lass."

Once I was within arm's reach, he pulled me between his legs.

"I know ye love me. I know ye would see me safe, but I'm a warrior first. The same trust that ye asked us to give ye ye must give to us."

"I know. I'll accept any punishment you choose to give me."

He hugged me, hard, then pulled back to thumb away my tears. "No more crying, wee one."

"Undress her," Wulfgar ordered. "We must prepare her."

"Muriel, tonight will test your bond with us."

"But...we share no bond."

"We share a bond of love. Ye will feel it." Fergus stripped me, and I leaned into his hands, grateful for his touch.

"You are a beautiful one." His hand stroked my belly.

"Almost ready?" Wulfgar asked.

"Not quite," Fergus said with a wicked smile, and bent

his head to my breast. "Muriel, keep your hands where they are or I will tie them."

He sucked on my nipples until they were peaked and swollen, sticking up as high as they would go. I clasped my hands behind my back to keep from gripping his shoulders, and he nodded when he was done.

"Very good. Whatever happens tonight, we need ye to trust us, and to obey."

"I will," I promised.

The door creaked open and I grabbed for Fergus' arm, but instead of Siebold and his gang, a blonde woman entered. The witch, Yseult.

"What is this?" I blurted before I could stop myself.

Fergus shifted my grip to his hand and squeezed it. "We asked her to come. Go to the bed and lie down now, sweetheart. This is your punishment and your test."

Heart pounding, I obeyed.

Wulfgar had me lay on my back with my legs bent and bottom close to the edge of the bed.

Yseult and Fergus murmured quietly together.

"Do ye think it's possible?" Fergus was asking as they approached me.

"Let me see her," the witch replied.

"Spread your legs farther apart," Wulfgar said to me.

With an inaudible whimper, I obeyed, planting my feet on the bed more than shoulder width apart.

"Good lass." They were staring right at my cunny, slick and made ready from Fergus' mouth on my breasts.

"Do not touch her," Wulfgar said. "that is only for her mates."

"Very well," the witch murmured. "I think that we can place them here, here, and here." She pointed to both of my nipples and between my legs.

Wulfgar nodded. "Make ready, then."

"What is happening, Fergus?" I whispered as the other two stepped away.

"Are ye brave, Muriel?"

"What?"

"Wulfgar says ye do not believe ye are brave."

"I-I—"

"When I first saw ye in the cage, what did ye do?"

"I don't remember."

"Ye spoke with me, and I asked if ye were afraid."

"I was afraid."

"Yes, but ye did not act it. Ye spoke with me, and when the other wolves might hunt me down, ye distracted them. Ye saved me, and your sister."

I said nothing.

"Ye have always been brave, wee one," he crooned, stroking my hair back from my face. "It is time ye realized it."

I caught his hand. "I want to be your mate."

"Ye are. Nothing will ever change that. Even if ye don't bond with us, we will never let ye go."

"Here we are," Yseult returned to the edge of the bed, squinted down at me. "We are ready."

I shifted my feet nervously, but Fergus and Wulfgar sat on either side of me. Wulfgar held up a slender metal bar.

"This is a needle we have washed clean. I will pierce your nipples with them, so you can wear a ring."

Fergus bent over me. "It will please us for ye to do so, Muriel. Ye can say no, if ye truly wish. But we want this. Will ye do it for us?"

I didn't trust my voice so I nodded.

"Wipe the area with the cloth dipped in the water of life," Yseult ordered. "It will clean the area."

Wulfgar washed my skin gently while I shivered and my nipple peaked further.

"It will be better to tie her down, so she does not flinch and hurt herself," the witch added.

"I'll hold her," Fergus took my wrists and held them so my arms stretched above my head.

"This will pinch but not hurt for long," Wulfgar told me.

"I'll distract ye," Fergus leaned down and pressed his lips to mine. It took a few licks before I opened my mouth to his clever tongue. He teased mine a moment before drawing away. "Ye ready?"

"Yes," I breathed.

"There's my brave girl," Wulfgar murmured. His thick fingers were so nimble as he placed the needle against my pink flesh.

"Kiss me, Muriel," Fergus ordered and covered my face with his.

When the needle pierced me, the sting went straight to my cunny, and I moaned into Fergus' mouth. When the kiss ended, I was panting.

"She likes pain," Yseult remarked. "And being over-powered."

"Perfect for us," Fergus said. I basked in the warmth in his voice and gaze.

"Now the the other," Wulfgar said, and Yseult handed Fergus another needle.

Wulfgar crouched close. "Look at me, Muriel."

Fergus had taken his hands away but I kept my arms above my head.

"The rings we will place in your nipples will remind you that you are our bride, our mate. Some days you will be naked but for them, and we will string a chain between them. Do you know what the rings represent?"

"No."

Fergus plumped my nipple between two of his fingers before wiping it with the cloth, but I didn't look away from Wulfgar's intense gaze. The giant warrior's lips were so soft and full, and his eyes kind under heavy brows. Had I ever thought him less than beautiful?

"Us, Muriel. You wear one ring for Fergus, and one for me. But you also will wear one for you. Do you know where?"

"No."

"Here." He cupped my dripping cunny, and I jerked once, and again as Fergus pierced my other nipple. This time, the pain melted away.

Wulfgar stroked my lower lips for a moment before brushing against the sensitive spot between them. Sighing, I lay my head back on the bed and closed my eyes to focus on the sensation. Wulfgar teased me close to climax and took his hand away.

"Look, Muriel." Fergus had threaded little gold rings at my nipples. They glinted in the firelight. My nipples still throbbed, but not with pain.

"We'll place a chain between them and lead ye by it." Fergus leaned close, his face flushed and eyes fixed on my adorned breasts.

"Do you wish me to place the next piercing?" Yseult asked.

"No. I will do it," Wulfgar said.

"Let me," Fergus countered.

"It is a tricky piercing," the witch warned. "Easy to make a mistake, and the flesh is very tender."

Fergus knelt between my legs. "I can do it. Muriel trusts me, do ye not?"

"I do," My voice quivered a little.

"Give me a fresh needle," Fergus demanded, but when he got it, he set it against his own nipple. "For ye, Muriel," he winked at me and pierced himself. "Tis nothing. Just a wee pinch."

"You should tie her down," Yseult said.

"No," Wulfgar stripped off his shirt before coming back to the bed. "I will hold her."

He sat behind on the bed and gathered me into his lap. As I lay back against his firm body, my bottom still right on the edge of the bed. Wrapping one muscled arm around me, he propped my legs over his knees. With my legs so wide, my cunny was on display for all to see. Fergus and the witch bent close, studying my center.

"Here." Yseult pointed. "The needle should go through there. Do you see? You must be careful not to hit the raised bud that is the source of much of her pleasure."

"It is very small," Fergus frowned.

"Small things are often powerful and important," she answered.

"Mmm," Wulfgar's lips came to my ear. "Like Muriel."

I turned my head, pressing against him.

"Are you nervous?"

"A little," I admitted.

His large hand came to cup my breast. His thumb hovered over my new piercing, but didn't tease.

"So brave and strong."

I shifted uneasily at the compliment, and his arm around my middle tightened.

"Give your fear to me. Let us protect you."

"Let's get ye ready, Muriel," Fergus knelt on the floor so his head was level with my cunny. With a cocky grin, he kissed my inner thigh, his beard tickling the sensitive skin.

"None of that now. We need ye to be still."

It's not fair," I wriggled as his mouth browsed slowly up to my sopping center. Wulfgar chuckled and secured me with both arms, while Fergus gripped my knees.

"Hush. This is your punishment," Wulfgar reminded me.

"Your little pleasure bud needs to be standing up for me. I'll see to that, but first I need to clean away some of your honey."

Starting at the bottom of my weeping slit, he dragged his tongue upwards, taking care to probe into every crevice. By the time he reached the top, I was gasping and digging my heels into the bed.

"You will be still," Wulfgar ordered. "Or we will tie you down. But first we will whip you."

My body pulsed, reaching for pleasure, but I forced myself to relax and accept Fergus' ministrations. He continued lapping at my cunny, each lick long and slow and torturous.

"That's it. Do not resist."

"Almost ready," Fergus' whole face was wet. He leaned in again to swirl his tongue around my most sensitive bundle of nerves.

"What are you doing?" My head lolled on Wulfgar's chest, but the rest of me did not move.

"He will place the piercing near your pleasure bud."

"Oh, goddess—"

"A ring will mark your most sensitive nub and rub against it all day. It will drive you mad, but you will not touch it. Only we will be allowed to play with it, though you may beg us not to. We want you desperate and needy for us."

Fergus put his whole mouth over my cunny, and swept his lips together. For a moment, he sucked on the very spot he would pierce. Just as I would climax, he took his head away and rose to make ready.

"Please," I gasped, my body thrumming with want. "Why are you doing this?"

"It pleases the beast to have you submit." Wulfgar resettled me in his lap, widening his legs and mine with them. "It pleases you, too. It is in your nature. So says the witch."

I'd forgotten the witch. Yseult stood at the table, a small smile on her lips.

"Magic always requires sacrifice, Muriel," she said.

"What sacrifice?" I asked as Fergus stood and came to me with the needle.

"You. Your magic requires your submission and your pain. Did I not mention that during our chat?" Yseult sounded bored, but her eyes were fixed on what Fergus' was doing between my legs.

The red-headed warrior had knelt again. I flinched as the cool cloth hit my flesh.

"Once the area is clean, you need to lift away the flesh from the area you will pierce," Yseult came close to instruct him. Fergus' tongue poked out a little as he prodded my folds. He and the witch fussed until I thought I might go mad.

Instead, I closed my eyes, took a deep breath, and let myself float. I was no more than a vessel, obedient and ready to be used by my masters.

"There."

The needle pushed through, but instead of a sting, heat poured through me.

"Now the ring," Fergus murmured, and it was done. He rose, a broad grin on his face.

"Well done, Muriel," Wulfgar said. His fingers stroked my knee. "You did well."

"May I see?" the witch asked, and moved only after the warriors gave her leave. She leaned close enough that I felt a puff of warm air on my nethers. "How interesting," she murmured.

"What is it?"

"Usually the piercings take some time to heal. But look, the flesh is no longer red or swollen."

"Is there pain, Muriel?" Wulfgar helped me to sit up, where I peered between my parted legs.

"No." Desire pulsed through me. Teetering on the edge of a climax, I took care not to touch my skin, only the metal. "It does not hurt."

"She's bonded to us." Fergus took a handful of my hair and tugged lightly. "She healed quickly. It's working."

"You have our gratitude, witch," Wulfgar said. "You may leave us, now, but we will not forget this service."

I sat exploring the piercings at my nipples. Desire pulsed through me, so strong my hands trembled.

Fergus came to explore them with me. "The fun of these piercings is that they mark the exact spot where a man should touch."

"Will a stranger be touching me?" I asked half in jest. My mates knew my body well enough.

"Naughty Muriel," Wulfgar said. "If any man touched you we'd rip off his hand. Your mates are pleased to see you wear this chain for us."

"Unless ye want us to share ye with the pack," Fergus whispered, a wicked light in his eye. "Lead ye before them naked, flog ye until ye cry out for cocks. Blindfold ye and make ye guess who filled ye. Wulfgar and me...or another."

"He jests," Wulfgar growled. The frightening sound reverberated through me, and my body clenched with delicious vibration. "We will not share you. Never."

Fergus moved my hands to cup my breasts. I sat there like a statue, offering myself to his touch. The heat that claimed my body at the final piercing built into an inferno.

"One more thing," Fergus said. With careful fingers, he threaded a tiny chain through each ring.

"This represents the bond between us," he told me. The chain formed a shining silver triangle between my cunny and breasts. "Ye belong to us, and we to ye. We are connected, all three."

Gripping the metal links draped between my breast, he tugged lightly, and led me forward with the new leash. I followed with alacrity, lest he pull my nipples.

Wulfgar shadowed me, his hands hovering at my waist in case I should fall.

Fergus tugged the chain. Heat suffused my body, pouring through me at three stinging points.

He released his grip, but my cunny pulsed. Fluid gushed from me, soaking the insides of my thighs.

"Enough," Wulfgar said when I started to wobble. "Release her."

Fergus did so. Unable to stand any more, I sank to my knees. My whole body was consumed with fire, need burning through me until there was nothing left. I was no longer Muriel, but an empty vessel ready to be filled with pleasure.

My head craned to look up at my mates. "Please."

"That's it. Beg."

I licked my lips. "I need you inside me. Both of you. Together."

Shucking his jerkin and leather breeches, Fergus presented me with his cock.

At the sight, my cunny clenched hard and I moaned.

"So hot for it," Fergus murmured.

"What is going on?" I panted as he advanced, cock bobbing in front of my eager lips. Heat engulfed me, sending a new wave of liquid dripping down my legs. "What is happening to me?"

Wulfgar wrapped my hair around his hand and drew my head back for a moment. "The mating heat, little one. It has finally claimed you."

He gave my hair enough slack to face Fergus' cock again, but not enough to reach it.

"Please," I breathed. "I need you."

"As we need you."

With his fist in my hair, Wulfgar pushed my head forward as Fergus thrust his hip I needed no encouragement.

Fergus' hand caught the chain and jerked it, gently. I groaned and he stepped back with a happy curse.

"Enough. I don't want her mouth."

"Come Muriel."

Eager hands lifted and bore me to the bed where Fergus sat first and had me straddle him.

I sank down onto his cock, hissing with satisfaction.

"And now mine," Wulfgar clamped a hand on the scruff of my neck, pushed me down as he oiled my ass. Thick fingers stretched me and then his cock probed my entrance.

I started shaking.

"You will not cum," Wulfgar said sternly.

My cunny spasmed around Fergus' cock even as he gave the order.

"Please—I cannot wait—"

"You will, or you won't cum again for a week. We will keep you in a cage in the corner, and feed you from a bowl on your hands and knees."

"Our wee pet," Fergus grinned. "She already wears a

leash." He took the chain between my breasts and set it between his teeth "She grows wet, hearing us speak of it." The coarse hair on his chest scraped my soft skin.

Wulfgar's cock slid into my ass. I was full, so full, and tight. My men could take me a thousand times and I would never get used to it.

Wulfgar snapped his hips, slamming me further onto Fergus' long rod.

"Oh no," I gasped.

"Denying us already?" Fergus jerked his chin up, pulling on the chain.

I cursed.

"Naughty one."

"Fuck me." I ordered, doing my best to rock my hips between them, while keeping my upper half still so the chain would not tug my nipples further.

"No," Wulfgar rumbled. His hand squeezed the back of my neck until my body went liquid with surrender. "You do not tell us what to do."

A whine escaped me, an animal sound. Fergus' eyes lit at his beast growled low in response.

They started moving, Fergus thrusting up from below while Wulfgar pounded me from behind.

Pounded between them, I went limp and surrendered. Satisfaction poured through me.

Teeth scraped at vulnerable skin at the base of my neck. Fergus reared up and bit my shoulder just as Wulfgar's canines pierced the other.

I cried out, writhing as ecstasy whipped through me like lightning, white hot and blinding. My body pulsed around my men's cocks. Both Fergus and Wulfgar groaned. At once their climaxes hit them, and I was caught in the maelstrom again, bowed between them like a reed before a gale. Curses and hot breath reached my ears, but their hands on my fragile skin were tender. "Muriel," they repeated my name like a dove greets the dawn, with hope and wonder. I sobbed out the last of my orgasm as they held me and pressed close, their cocks rooted deep inside me as if they wished to live there for all time.

"I never knew it could be like this," Fergus panted.

"Pleasure like this has not been, nor will ever be anywhere but in Muriel's arms. It is heaven beyond my imagining."

At Wulfgar's awed and humbled tone, I turned my head and kissed him.

When I drew away, he thumbed wet from my cheek. Tears still leaked from my eyes.

"I feel you." I touched my heart, where pleasure still hummed through me. "Is it the bond?"

"It is," Wulfgar lay his hand over mine. "It was waiting. All it required was surrender."

I touched my shoulders where the wounds had healed to a neat pair of red marks.

"The pack will see this, and know I am yours. Will they still make Fergus fight?"

Fergus gripped my other hands. "Ye will not worry about such things. Let your mates take care of ye."

"You're ours. Bond or no, we will never let you go."

A WEIGHT LEFT my side and I came awake. Wulfgar had risen and started to leave the bed.

I rolled and caught his arm.

"Don't go," I mumbled. Beside me Fergus snored.

Wulfgar bent close to whisper. "I'm not, little one. I only go to see to the fire."

After building up the blaze, he returned and settled next to me.

Safe between my two mates, I melted into sleep.

VOICES ECHOED in my head before I opened my eyes. Fergus sat beside me on the bed, honing a blade. Wulfgar drank a horn by the fire. Neither spoke, yet I heard their voices in my head.

Watch his left arm, Wulfgar lectured. *He favors his right but has been known to feint and deal great blows with his lesser arm.*

I'm more concerned about his followers. They will not face me one by one, the cowards.

Strike Siebold down and they will scatter like rabbits, Wulfgar's voice sounded rich and content.

"How do you do that?" I asked.

They glanced at me, startled as if they hadn't known I was awake.

"Do what, sweetheart?"

"Speak without your lips moving."

"Ye can hear us?" Fergus asked with shock. Wulfgar came to my side and I sat up between them.

"Yes. I hear you clearly. Well," I frowned, recalling the echoing voice. "Very faintly, but the words are there." I frowned. The words sometimes seemed to be only pictures, impressions of feelings. Joy pulsed through me now, its origin the two men sitting beside me.

"That's it, Muriel. That is the bond."

I blinked at them. I'd been hearing them since the very beginning.

"Ye have?" Fergus burst out, and I realized I'd spoken my very thought into their minds.

Yes. I spoke into the path between us.

"What did you hear, Muriel?"

"You said that Siebold might try to test our bond. It was one of the first nights we were together."

The warriors exchanged a look.

"You've been hearing us all this time," Wulfgar shook his head. "If we'd known we'd have hidden our thoughts more carefully."

"We dinnae want ye to worry. The Alphas gave us counsel to let the bond form on its own."

"The bond forms naturally, when there's love."

Love, not fear. The witch had tried to tell me all along.

"That's it then," I reared up, and flung my arms around Fergus. "You do not have to fight Siebold."

"Aye, lass," he accepted my kiss, "I dinnae have to, but I want to."

"What? Fergus, you cannot—"

"I need to do this." He set me away when I would cling to him. Wulfgar gathered me into his lap.

"Let your mate do as he needs, Muriel. Have faith in him. The faith of a woman can do wonders to a man's strength."

"I do not wish to see you killed."

"I will not be killed." He tapped my nose, jovial for a man about to fight. "Trust me."

9

I held in my outburst until we were halfway up the mountain. Fergus led the way and Wulfgar walked behind me. I wore a silky dress that left my arms bare and a wreath of white flowers on my head. My hair was unbound.

My steps slowed when Wulfgar caught me around the hips.

"Are your legs weary, Muriel?"

"No." But I couldn't make them move.

Fergus grinned back at me. "Do ye wish me to carry ye over my shoulder? 'Twill be a fine sight, but it might muss your wee crown." He plucked a flower from my headdress. I swatted him halfheartedly.

"What's wrong, Muriel?"

"I fear for you."

Wulfgar wrapped his arm around my waist and lifted me, carrying me off the path into the forest. Once there, he set me down in front of a lichen-covered boulder. "Place your hands on the rock, Muriel."

"What—"

He tipped me forward. Before I could protest, my dress was up at my waist and he'd swatted my bottom.

"Ow!"

"Hands," he ordered, and when I obeyed, "now bend at the waist and spread your legs. Feet wide. Wider."

"Good lass." Fergus approached holding up the plug for my bottom. "We wondered when ye would speak up in fear. If you'd waited much longer, we would have had to put the plug in before the whole pack. Don't worry, we will find a way to distract your troubled mind."

I sighed but let him twist the plug into my bottom.

"There." They let me rise and pull my dress back down. I pressed my legs together. My juices already began to drip.

"Must I wear the plug?"

"You must. 'Tis good for ye to remember your submission to your mates. Trust me, lass. After the fight, I will be the one to take it out."

I crossed my arms over my chest, where the metal of my piercings showed through the thin fabric of my gown.

"Are you sure I can go before the pack like this?"

"Ye are our mate, and beautiful. It does the pack good to see it. Besides, we are your mates, and none dare challenge us."

"Siebold dared," I grumbled, but let Fergus tug my hands down.

"After today, no one will."

"Though your scent will make them mad with wanting," Wulfgar said.

"What?" I hadn't even thought about my scent.

"Be at ease," Fergus said. "He only jests. Poorly." And the red-head stuck out his tongue at the giant.

"Put that thing away, or I'll tear it out," Wulfgar threatened.

"You willnae. Muriel will miss it too much. She enjoyed it quite a few times last night."

I gasped. "Fergus!"

"'Tis true."

As we grew close, our joking mood fell away.

The entire pack waited for us at the top of the mountain.

An unearthly wind blew through the clearing, lifting my hair away from my shoulders. The whole pack could see the small claiming scars on my neck.

I forced myself to keep from hunching or crossing my arms over the bare shelf of chest that showed my cleavage.

Let us help you. My mates spoke into my mind in eerie unison, and both took one of my hands in theirs.

We walked side by side to the center of the circle.

Samuel waited on his throne, and Daegan standing beside.

Siebold also waited with a knot of warriors at his back.

"Well met, Muriel of Alba," he said to me.

Why does he speak to me?

He insults us by not acknowledging us, your mates.

Raising my chin, I looked the bully straight in the eye.

His widened. "You dare look at me?"

"Yes," I said. "I do. You could challenge me if you like. Here are my champions." I nodded to the grim warriors on either side of me.

My mates hands tightened on mine, but they didn't chastise me.

"One of your champions is the smallest and weakest of the pack."

Fergus tugged me to face him. "I am small," he told me, "but I am fast, and I have my wits, and the strength of my warrior brother. Do I have your favor."

"Yes." I rose to tiptoe and touched his lips with mine.

"Remember. Tonight, I am the one who removes the plug."

I flushed. There were many pairs of ears in the clearing, and all of them had heard Fergus' promise. He could've chosen to speak to me via the bond.

Where's the fun in that? He tugged my hair and strode into the middle of the wolves.

"I'm ready, Alphas."

Siebold still stared at me. I now ignored him, still as a statue even when the cold wind picked up and raised goose-bumps on my bare arms. Wulfgar wrapped the great fur cloak he wore around my shoulders.

"Enough," Wulfgar growled. "No more looking at my mate."

"I just wanted to ask her how she fared last night, lying with a murderer."

"We are all murderers, Siebold." Wulfgar's finger brushed my cheek. "Muriel has forgiven me."

"She does not know who you truly are."

"I do, my love," I spoke to Wulfgar, who bent down so our foreheads almost touched. Though I whispered the next words, I knew the entire pack heard us. "I am bonded to you and I know you will never hurt me." I smoothed a hand over his close shaven head and rested my hand on the back of his neck. "Siebold is jealous because no woman would ever choose him over you."

Wulfgar grinned and winked at me before he raised his head. "Do you hear that, Siebold?"

The blond bully snarled.

"If not, I'll tell him again," I raised my voice. "You're a monster, Siebold. A good thing you never had a chance of winning the Games. Any woman would throw herself off the mountain before she lay with you."

"You'll pay for that. Like the whore who chose him over me. It was the last decision she ever made."

An image flashed in my head and I spoke before I knew I'd opened my mouth, "You killed her, Siebold. Snapped her neck while Wulfgar slept, at peace. But you will never know peace. Your beast never sleeps. It stirs you to violence again and again. You live and will die by its rage."

A murmur rippled around the pack. "Volva," I heard one Berserker whisper.

What is 'Volva'? I asked my men silently.

A witch, a prophetess, they answered.

My prophecy seemed to anger Siebold all the more. He pointed at Wulfgar.

"Watch your back, Enforcer."

"He doesn't have to. I watch it for him," Fergus spoke.

Siebold whirled to answer, and his face met Fergus' fist. The bully's head snapped back, but he quickly regained his feet, pushing forward with a roar. The pack came alive, men whooping and shouting, wolves snarling. The two fighters danced around each other. Fergus was a head shorter than the blond, but fast. He whipped around the larger warrior, only to stagger when Siebold caught him with his fist. The smaller warrior rolled with the punch and grabbed his shield and sword while he was down.

One of Siebold's cronies tossed him his axe.

"I made him angry," I whispered to Wulfgar, pressing against his great chest.

"It is good, little one. Angry wolves do not think clearly. Siebold will make mistakes."

But as the fight went on, it became clear why Siebold was one of the most dominant wolves in the pack. He drove forward, and his blows rang out on Fergus' shield, hard enough to vibrate in my bones.

I could only imagine how they jarred Fergus' shield arm. Again and again, Siebold struck, driving Fergus to the ground under his superior weight.

Finally, Fergus threw the shield and weapon away.

"No," I cried out, but Wulfgar's arms around me tightened.

I could not stay and do nothing, but I could not go. I could not hide my face. There was nothing I could do.

"Ready to meet your end sooner?"

"I should've done this a long time ago. I will not face ye as all the others have."

"You will not match me, strength to strength?"

"Strength comes in many forms. I choose to beat ye—by my wits."

The last word rang out as a bark as Fergus Changed into the red wolf.

"What is happening?" I clutched at Wulfgar.

"He's in wolf form. It's a lesser form, it is allowed."

Lithe and quick, teeth flashing, the red wolf danced around the warrior. The axe came down but the wolf was never there.

"He wears him out," Wulfgar told me.

At one pass, the wolf darted close to Siebold's legs. The blond cried out and staggered.

"First blood, Fergus."

The wolf dodged the axe and its teeth caught Siebold's arm.

He kept coming and darting, driving the larger warrior across the clearing.

"You can cut me a thousand times, runt. I will not die. I heal."

Fergus rushed, tripping him and twisting to clamp on

his leg. The wolf dragged the warrior across the fighting area.

"Good move. Our Red bites his heel. The wound bleeds much and will not heal quickly. See? He is limping."

With a wind that prickled my skin, Fergus transformed back into a man. He raced to the edge of the circle where he'd left his weapons, and leaped at Siebold with sword in hand. The blond managed to get his axe up in time to block the blow. Next, the sword and shield fell to the ground and he faced a raging red wolf.

"How did Fergus Change so quickly?"

Wulfgar's arms loosened around me, his chest rising and falling faster.

He drew on your strength? I asked merging my mind to his, all at once I heard them speaking to one another, echoes sounding like the instructions Fergus gave me when we were sparring. This time the orders were in Wulfgar's voice.

Watch his left arm. He raises it when he is going to feint.

Siebold trudged forward, swiping his axe at the swift wolf.

Why doesn't Siebold also Change into the wolf?

He is not so quick. He saves his strength for the fight at the end, when the Alpha's allow them to take beast form.

I bit my lip. The red wolf was quick, but Siebold was so much larger. How did Fergus stand a chance?

"Have faith in him, Muriel," Wulfgar said. He had caught the echo of my thought. As grunts and the clang of weapons rang out across the clearing, I closed my eyes. Fergus' face, split with a grin, waited for me. Fergus laughing. Fergus looking through the bars of the cage. Teaching me to fight. Promising in front of the whole pack to see to me tonight.

The pack had fallen eerily quiet.

"Last quarter," Samuel called. "Beast form."

Win for me, Fergus. I am waiting.

Slowly the Change took the red wolf, rolling up through his hind paws and ending at the tip of his monstrous muzzle, pointed high in the sky.

I gasped. Fergus' beast was ten feet tall, at least a head and half taller than Siebold. Above me, Wulfgar grinned.

See, little one? I told you.

"Why--?" I opened and closed my mouth.

"Why didn't he win the Games? He didn't have to. We agreed he'd lend his strength to me. Besides, my guess is his new power is a surprise to him as much as it is to everyone else."

Fergus looked down at his giant, razor tipped paws, then at Siebold's smaller monster with dirty blond fur. The red beast grinned.

Siebold rushed forward, trailing blood from his ankle. Fergus dodged, and dodged again when Siebold came a second time.

Wulfgar chuckled. "He still fights like the little wolf."

Siebold rushed forward, and feinted, but he was too slow. Fergus caught his side with a blow and the blond staggered.

Another blow, and Siebold fell. The fourth strongest warrior in the pack slammed onto his back in the dust. Fergus drove the sword through his shoulder, pinning him to the ground.

That's twice we've spared your life, Siebold. It will not happen a third time. Fergus' voice echoed loudly through the pack bonds.

With a grunt, the beast whirled and pointed at me. "Mine."

I stepped forward when light flashed in my eyes, glinting

off two blades. Siebold's two cronies closed in behind Fergus.

"Fergus," I screamed, out loud and in my mind. My redheaded mate turned, arms up to fend off the blow. I tried to shout, but my voice was too hoarse.

I pushed my mind into my mates, rising to tiptoes as I drew on power.

No!

The word rang out into the silence, an echo in my head. My ears rang from the large boom, loud as a crack of thunder.

In the whole clearing, my mates and I were the only ones standing. Every wolf and Berserker was flat on the ground, floundering like stranded fishes.

Samuel slouched on his throne, gripping the sides as if he would have tumbled off completely. Lines of strain marred his face. He beckoned to my mates. Quickly Wulfgar led me before him, clasping my shoulders when I would've swayed on my feet. "Did you draw on her power to win this fight?"

Fergus was back in man form. He looked a little dazed. "I think so."

"Either that, or she drew on ours," Wulfgar answered for him.

Samuel thought this over, then gestured to Daegan, who raised his voice, "It has been decided. The victor is clear. Fergus has beaten off all challengers. Both he and Wulfgar have taken Muriel to mate."

Wulfgar took Fergus' hand and joined it with mine. "She is yours. Fairly won."

Turning, I grabbed both my warrior's hands.

Come, I urged, speaking directly to their minds. *Let's go home.*

The ringing in my ears didn't leave until we were halfway to the cabin.

"By the moon, what was that?" Fergus asked in an awestruck tone.

Wulfgar laughed. "The witch said Muriel had powers."

I SHOOK my head to clear it. "I don't think that's what she meant."

"Whatever it was, it worked," Fergus shook his head. His ears were still ringing, but other than that he was no worse for wear. Blood marred his skin, his wounds had already healed.

A weight lifted off me, and I gave Wulfgar a sly look. "Perhaps I will call Yseult, and ask her."

"If you do, we'll ask her where else we might pierce your flesh and add a ring to lead you."

I blushed.

"Perhaps her lower lips," Fergus mused. "We could thread a thong between the rings, and knot it shut so she cannot touch. Then only take her arse and mouth, till she begs us for relief."

"A fine idea. I think the hope of pleasure will keep her sweet. There are metal belts she can wear, an armor we can lock over her cunny until we allow it off."

I gasped. "I will not submit to such a thing."

"Ye have no choice, Muriel. You're ours to see to as we please. Ye heard the Alphas." Fergus grinned.

I swatted his arm, and Wulfgar clapped me on the bottom, hard enough to send me forward a few paces.

"Is that anyway to treat your true mate?" I pouted. Inspired, I strode ahead of them and stopped.

The men waited, curious as to what I would do.

"This walk is taking too long," I said. "Let's have a game."

Fergus' head tilted and Wulfgar's chin raised, predators scenting prey at the start of the hunt. "What sort of game, wee one?"

I tugged my gown over my head, followed by my shift, and let both garments fall. A thrill went through me as I saw the beast leap into their eyes. "A race? Winner takes my ass," I suggested, before I turned tail and ran.

For more Berserkers, read Brenna's book <u>Sold to the Berserkers</u>, Sabine's book <u>Taken by the Berserkers</u>, or Fleur's book Claimed by the Berserkers

FREE BOOK

Get two secret Berserker books, Bred by the Berserkers and
A Berserker Birth, available exclusively to you:

A NOTE FROM LEE SAVINO

Hey there. It's me, Lee Savino. I'm so glad you read this book and ordered it directly from my store. Readers like you make my author life possible! And being an author is a dream come true.

If you're like me, you're wondering what to read next. Let me help you out...

If you haven't yet, check out the two exclusive extras I wrote in the Berserker world. They're available here:

Bred by the Berserkers
https://geni.us/BredBerserkerNONL

A Berserker Birth
https://geni.us/BirthBerserkerNONL

And if you want more Berserkers, you can find the complete selection at my store or get the 15 book bundle here!

WANT MORE BERSERKERS?

These fierce warriors will stop at nothing to claim their mates...

Get a 15 e-book Berserker bundle on sale at my Lee Savino shop!

The Berserker Saga

Sold to the Berserkers – Brenna, Samuel & Daegan
Mated to the Berserkers – Brenna, Samuel & Daegan
Bred by the Berserkers (FREE novella only available to you) – Brenna, Samuel & Daegan
Taken by the Berserkers – Sabine, Ragnvald & Maddox
Given to the Berserkers – Muriel and her mates
Claimed by the Berserkers – Fleur and her mates
Rescued by the Berserker – Hazel & Knut
Captured by the Berserkers – Willow, Leif & Brokk
Kidnapped by the Berserkers – Sage, Thorbjorn & Rolf
Bonded to the Berserkers – Laurel, Haakon & Ulf

Berserker Babies – the sisters Brenna, Sabine, Muriel, Fleur
and their mates
Night of the Berserkers – the witch Yseult's story
Owned by the Berserkers – Fern, Dagg & Svein
Tamed by the Berserkers — Sorrel, Thorsteinn & Vik
Mastered by the Berserkers — Juliet, Jarl & Fenrir
Surrendered to the Berserkers — Rosalind and her mates

Berserker Warriors

Ægir *(formerly titled The Sea Wolf)*
Siebold with Ines Johnson

ALSO BY LEE SAVINO

For film and TV rights inquiries: <u>lee.savino@leesavino.com</u>

Paranormal romance

Berserker Saga

Sold to the Berserkers

Mated to the Berserkers

Bred by the Berserkers (FREE novella only available at
www.leesavino.com)

Taken by the Berserkers

Given to the Berserkers

Claimed by the Berserkers

Rescued by the Berserker

Captured by the Berserkers

Kidnapped by the Berserkers

Bonded to the Berserkers

Berserker Babies

Night of the Berserkers

Owned by the Berserkers

Tamed by the Berserkers

Mastered by the Berserkers

Surrendered to the Berserkers

Midnight Doms with Renee Rose

Alpha's Blood

His Captive Mortal

The Virgin and the Vampire

(All Souls' Night anthology exclusive)

Werewolves of Wallstreet with Renee Rose

Big Bad Boss: Midnight

Big Bad Boss: Moon Mad

~

Sci fi romance

Planet of Kings with Tabitha Black

Brutal Mate

Brutal Claim

Brutal Capture

Brutal Beast

Brutal Demon

Tsenturion Warriors with Golden Angel

Alien Captive

Alien Tribute

Alien Abduction

Dragons in Exile with Lili Zander

Draekon Mate

Draekon Fire

Draekon Heart

Draekon Abduction

Draekon Destiny

Daughter of Draekons

Draekon Fever

Draekon Rogue

Draekon Holiday

Draekon Rebel Force with Lili Zander

Draekon Warrior

Draekon Conqueror

Draekon Pirate

Draekon Warlord

Draekon Guardian

Contemporary Romance

Royally Bad

Royally Fake Fiancé

Her Marine Daddy

Her Dueling Daddies

Beauty & The Lumberjacks

Snowed in with the Lumberjack

Rescuing Regina

Dark Mafia Romance

Mafia Brides

Revenge is Sweet

Vengeance is Mine

A Dark Mafia Romance trilogy with Stasia Black

Innocence

Awakening

Queen of the Underworld

Beauty and the Rose trilogy with Stasia Black

Beauty's Beast

Beauty & the Thorns

Beauty & the Rose

Cowboy Romance

Rocky Mountain Mail Order Brides

Rocky Mountain Dawn

Rocky Mountain Bride

Rocky Mountain Rose

Rocky Mountain Romp

Rocky Mountain Rogue

Rocky Mountain Daddy

Rocky Mountain Ride

Possessing Pearl

Wild Whip Ranch with Tristan River

Cowboy's Babygirl

Taming His Wild Girl

ABOUT THE AUTHOR

USA today bestselling author Lee Savino has written over 69 steamy romance novels. Bad boys, mafia men, wolf shifters, and dragon shifters in space—her dominant, alpha-hole heroes will stop at nothing to possess their one true love. Happily-ever-after and book hangover guaranteed!

Connect with Lee Savino in her fabulous Goddess Group:
https://www.facebook.com/groups/LeeSavino